THE Pirate Rebel

The Story of Notorious Ned Jordan

Elizabeth Peirce

NIMBUS
PUBLISHING LTD

For my mother, Cyril, and Terry, with love.

Nimbus Publishing Limited
PO Box 9166, Halifax, NS B3K 5M8
(902) 455-4286   www.nimbus.ns.ca

Printed and bound in Canada

Interior Design: Kathy Kaulbach
Author photo: Ian Guppy

Image credits:
Chapter start page image: Courtesy of Nova Scotia Archives and Records Managment,
Page 156 (top): Courtesy of Nova Scotia Museum, History Collection
Page 156 (bottom): Courtesy of Maritime Museum of the Atlantic, Gerry Lunn

Library and Archives Canada Cataloguing in Publication
        Peirce, Elizabeth, 1975-
        The pirate rebel : the story of notorious Ned Jordan / Elizabeth Peirce.
        ISBN 978-1-55109-624-7

1. Jordan, Ned, d. 1809—Fiction. 2. Piracy—Nova Scotia—History—19th century—Fiction. 3. Pirates—Nova Scotia—Biography—Fiction. I. Title.
PS8581.E3929P57 2007   C813'.6   C2007-904585-5

NOVA SCOTIA
Tourism, Culture and Heritage

We acknowledge the financial support of the Government of Canada through the Book Publishing Industry Development Program (BPIDP) and the Canada Council, and of the Province of Nova Scotia through the Department of Tourism, Culture and Heritage for our publishing activities.

Author's Note & Acknowledgements

"Justice, though slow, is sure—
Vengeance o'ertakes the swiftest villain's guilt."

(from Royal Gazette, November 14, 1809, Halifax, NS)

I N WRITING THIS STORY, I have relied on Archibald MacMechan's account of the murders on board *Three Sisters*, entitled "Jordan the Pirate," contained in his *Sagas of the Sea* (London: J.M. Dent and Sons, 1923) as well as on the information contained in Gerald Stairs' unpublished manuscript, "The Stairs of Halifax" (1962). Other information on the trial of Edward and Margaret Jordan appeared in the contemporary Halifax newspapers *The Royal Gazette* and *The Novator* (1809). Information on Halifax's celebration of Prevost's Martinique expedition was found in volume 22 of the 1809 *Naval Chronicle*.

Special thanks to Dan Conlin of the Maritime Museum of the Atlantic, for elucidating the finer points of a sea chase and for providing details about Halifax in the early nineteenth century, and to Sandra McIntyre and Penelope Jackson of Nimbus Publishing for their helpfulness. In its final stages, the book owes much to Kelsey McLaren and Heather Bryan at Nimbus, Anjali Vohra at NSARM, and Ian Guppy. While the author has aimed for historical accuracy whenever possible in the recounting of Jordan's story, many characters and events in this book are purely and necessarily fictional.

Chapter 1

*"We shall no longer walk over fields
stained with the blood of our ancestors."*
(Resolution of the Society of United Irishmen)

August 1797, County Carlow, Ireland—

Ned Jordan woke from a nightmare with the frightening sensation of being suffocated, his hands grasping frantically at his throat where he could still feel the tightness of the noose. Once his breath had returned, he looked about him, half-surprised at the absence of the gallows; he was, in fact, still lying in the hay loft of John Byrne's barn, the slumbering Brennan's comfortable warmth beside him.

Jordan rose slowly, brushing the prickly hay from his old coat, and climbed down from the loft. The sun had not yet risen and he shivered in the damp and clammy darkness.

It was the third time in a week that he had been visited by the nightmare, and each visit revealed to him more horrifying details. The setting was a small rocky beach at the mouth of a bay Jordan had never seen. From this vantage point, Jordan could clearly see across a narrow sea-passage to the shore of a nearby island where four wizened figures, blackened by tar, swung by their necks like crazy scarecrows from the high beam of a gallows. On the opposite shore, Jordan was being led to a gallows he knew had been made just for him in a screaming southeast wind, accompanied by a faceless priest who mumbled the words of the last rites of the Roman Catholic church, the tails of his black robe billowing out like bats' wings. Surrounding the place of execution stood a silent crowd of citizens watching Jordan with grim faces as he mounted the thirteen steps to the gallows platform and placed the noose around his own neck.

Jordan gazed out to sea, where the breakers crashed over a distant shoal. The wind howled around him with a murderous strength. His last sight was of a ship, a schooner, maybe, approaching the beach at a supernatural rate of speed, coming straight at him. He tried to scream but the platform dropped beneath his feet just as the schooner ran aground on the beach with a terrible grinding sound.

All three versions of the dream had ended the same way and had not lost any of their horror for repetition.

JORDAN KNEW the reason for the nightmare. It was the end of summer, 1797, he was Catholic, and he had taken the oath of loyalty of the United Irishmen, an act of defiance against the government of Ireland that was punishable by death. The brotherhood, as it was called, despised the well-to-do landowners who now lorded over the most fertile acreage of Ireland, charging poor farmers exorbitant rents on portions of land that could never sustain them. These landlords lived in splendour while their tenants huddled in squalid cottages barely kept warm with smoky peat fires. England and its Anglo-Irish lackeys had taken enough, more than enough, from Ireland; it was time for governance of the country to be returned to its rightful owners, those who worked the land.

All this Ned Jordan had solemnly sworn, together with William Brennan, the Byrne boys and many of the young men Jordan had grown up with. Protestants or Catholics, tenant-farmers in the country, day-labourers and shopkeepers in the towns—these things made no difference to the brotherhood. Fitzgerald had been a lord, a member of the Anglo-Irish elite, but when he took his oath, he had dramatically renounced his title. And now with Wolfe

Tone in France in negotiation with Napoleon's lieutenants, players in the great revolutionary drama of nine years earlier, it would not be long before a French fleet crossed the Channel and an invading force pushed their common English enemy out of Ireland forever.

Jordan opened the barn door and stood in the doorway, his arms folded tightly across his chest against the chill. The familiar expanse of pastureland before him was indistinct in the grey half-light of before dawn, and he was still shaken by the dream landscape he had only just escaped. It was a relief to witness the rising of the sun, to see the pasture regain its daytime familiarity, to hear the sounds of the animals stirring in the barn and Brennan's drawn-out throat-clearing as he dislodged the straw dust from his lungs and sent an impressive gob of spit sailing from the loft to the barn floor, landing scant inches from where Jordan stood.

Turning back toward the loft with disgust, Jordan's voice conveyed his fury: "Mind your aim, for the love of God, or I've a mind to turn you in to the first rackrentin' bastard crosses my path!"

Brennan looked startled. "Ned—I thought you was gone out."

"Well, I weren't, as you may plainly see."

"John's Bridey will have our breakfast by now," said Brennan with expectation in his voice, as he climbed down from the loft and joined Jordan on the barn floor. "I'm half-starved."

A lamb that had wiggled its way out of its stall skipped past the two men and made for the open barn door.

"No, you don't," said Jordan, grabbing the animal under its belly and heaving it unceremoniously back inside, while it bleated indignantly. "You tell Bridget I'll be along presently. I'm going to pay a call to the Byrne boys; we'll be needing them for the drill tonight."

"Suit yourself, Ned. You know what a temper Bridey has when her meals are left to go cold on the table. I'll not be held responsible—if you come back and find your plate cleaned, you'll know I did it only to spare you her wrath."

Jordan found Brennan's passion for eating repulsive, his own lean frame a testament to the moderation he exercised at table.

Brennan ambled past him and down the dirt path leading to John and Bridget Byrne's small stone cottage, where wisps of smoke escaped from the chimney. Jordan saw him as far as the kitchen door, then turned and made his way toward town and the house where the seventeen-year-old twins Paddy and Toby Byrne, John's nephews, lived. It was a good two miles' walk, and Jordan kept a brisk pace. The breeze ruffled the young man's black hair, and his thick black brows were furrowed in thought. He had not shaved in several days, and the beginnings of a thick black beard covered his cheeks and chin, giving him an unkempt appearance. He felt the pistol snug beneath his arm, a weapon he had acquired when he had taken his oath. Earlier this year, he had left Dublin for the country and had begun training for the uprising planned for the following spring, already being referred to among the oath-takers as the "Glorious '98." The invading French fleet would need ground support, and concerted uprisings were quietly being planned for all of Ireland's major centres, with Dublin as the main prize. Once the occupying English forces realized the magnitude of the undertaking, it would only be a matter of time before they agreed to terms with the rebels and their French allies and the rebellion would be over. The success of the United Irishmen's momentous enterprise hung on two crucial factors: training and secrecy.

As Jordan approached the Byrne boys' house, he felt, not for the first time, the sharp teeth of self-doubt gnawing at the storehouse of his resolve. A tolerably good marksman, he had volunteered to train the two young men in the basics of combat, something he actually knew little about. The Byrnes were poor and could not afford weapons other than homemade pikes and clubs. Would these be enough to repulse a well-armed English army?

The boys' father made a meagre living growing barley on land belonging to the haughty landowner Henry Breckenridge, who spent much of his time in London; Byrne paid the greater share of the profits he received from the grain to his landlord in exchange for use of the land. Breckenridge had already informed the Byrnes that he planned on enclosing acres now under cultivation to pasture sheep, leaving the family on the brink of starvation. The twins had nursed a hatred for Breckenridge since they were old enough to be aware of their father's plight, and were some of the first young men in the county to enlist with the United Irishmen, with their father's knowledge and blessing. They relished their nighttime drills in the woods behind their uncle's barn and the opportunity to meet like-minded men, such as Ned Jordan. They knew he had come to the farm from Dublin some weeks ago and would be staying at John's place until the uprising should take place; of his life before the brotherhood, no one seemed to know. Jordan had made vague references to being a shopkeeper's apprentice in his teens, but never talked about having a shop of his own nor of any business dealings, past or present. To the Byrnes, Jordan's silence about his past and his frequent moodiness only added to his mystique.

The twins were threshing in the fields when they spotted Jordan's dark figure approaching. Gratefully dropping their scythes, they rushed out to greet him.

"Brother Ned! We had not expected you so early—come inside, do. Mother will put the kettle on."

Before Jordan could reply, Paddy Byrne had pinned his arms behind his back, and with good humour, propelled him toward the cottage.

Jordan smiled at the exuberance that came so easily to the Byrnes.

"Good God—will you serve the army so when they march against us at Dublin?" he asked half-jokingly as he was marched to the kitchen door.

"Give me a pike and I'll knock the bastards' brains out!" Paddy replied with fervour.

Jordan could see that the training was having an effect—two weeks ago, the boy would never have been able to seize him in such a way. He felt slightly uneasy—how simple it was to turn well-meaning boys into killers! He kept this sentiment to himself, and spoke instead the words he knew the brotherhood would want him to say: "You do me proud, Padraig—our country is the better for men like you and your brother."

Paddy let go of his teacher's arms and, seized with sudden feeling, crossed himself.

"God bless you, Ned! God bless Ireland!"

September 1797, Halifax, Nova Scotia—

AS HE SPLASHED WATER on his face and prepared for school, John Stairs' attention was drawn through the window to the bustle of activity on the wharves just beyond the windows of his uncle's house at 13 Lower Water Street. A forest of masts from every kind of vessel attracted his eye—fishing schooners loading gear from the chandlery or unloading cod in barrels, small craft perhaps belonging to the inhabitants of the tiny communities south of town in for supplies or a pleasant excursion. Sometimes, he saw a British frigate en route to the careening yard in the north end of town, a sight that reminded him of the war with France being fought on the other side of the Atlantic. War ships were on the minds of most Haligonians these days, since the majestic *Tribune*, taken the year before from the French in a great sea battle, had only recently been wrecked in the approaches to the harbour with great loss of life, through the negligence of a stubborn English captain who refused the services of a pilot.

John Stairs admired the war ships, though he had no desire to serve in the Royal Navy, where discipline and brutality were often indistinguishable. He and his younger brother William had lately witnessed a sailor convicted of desertion being flogged around the fleet at anchor in the harbour.

"When will they stop?" eight-year-old Willy had asked with quiet horror in his voice.

"Not 'til he stops breathing," John had replied with a nonchalance he did not feel. In truth, the twelve-year-old longed to go to sea, but never as an unfortunate regular seaman, recruited against his will by the press gangs who periodically swept the streets of Halifax clean of men for their ships. No, it was the merchant navy that captured his imagination—the wide-bottomed ships that brought goods to so many shops along the waterfront: rum, sugar and molasses from Jamaica, flour from New England, linens and china from the British Isles. When would his uncle Stayner realize that continuing at school only sharpened his desire for escape, to see the world beyond the narrow confines of the garrison town of Halifax? Ruefully, John reflected that if his father were around, he would surely understand his son's plight and not insist that he continue his needless studies at the Grammar School.

But John Stayner had promised his brother-in-law, John and William's father, that he would see to their education until the boys were old enough to choose a trade and be taken on as apprentices

It was their father's dying wish for his two sons. Now, the Stairs children were orphans. An epidemic of yellow fever had claimed their mother Joanna when she and her family were visiting friends in Philadelphia four summers ago. Young John had been the only one of his four siblings to attend her burial; bravely, he had stood next to his weeping father as her grave was filled with earth. He could not cry. When his father, then aged forty-five, married a woman not much older than John's oldest sister, six weeks after their mother's death, no one was surprised except the children.

"A man must have a wife," his father had explained to young John at the wedding, "and you need a mother."

John never thought of Susannah Stairs as a mother, though she treated the children well enough. She quickly had a child of her own, though, and even John could not blame her for preferring her own flesh and blood to her husband's older children.

It had only been a few months since his father's death, and John still felt alone in the world. The five Stairs children had been taken in by their mother's people, the Stayners, but the house on Water Street was crowded with the children of the two families, and with three Johns in the house, the twelve-year-old was frequently lost in the shuffle.

When he was captain of a merchant vessel plying the South Seas trade, there would be no confusion about his place in the world!

John Stairs was determined to make a name for himself in his profession. For now, his greatest concern, though, was to find his cap and coat among the regiment of clothing hung on hooks at the door. He searched impatiently for several minutes; they were not to be found. With a sigh, he grabbed the nearest substitutes from a hook and passed through the door and onto Water Street.

October 1797, County Carlow—

"HIGHER! Aim higher, lad!"

Toby Byrne straightened his right arm and squinted at the target that seemed a great distance away, Jordan's pistol in his hand. His brother stood next to him, smiling at the turnip Jordan had placed on top of two overturned barrels in an empty field and told them to pretend was the head of King George.

"That's right, Toby—take your time and get him in your sights, then give it to him right between the eyes!" said Jordan with a bitter laugh.

The shot scared the birds in the little copse near the barn; they flew skywards in a sudden burst of flight. The turnip, though, remained safely on its perch.

"Ha! You'll not unseat the English bastard that way," laughed Paddy, seizing the weapon roughly from his brother's hand. "Leave the job to a true Irish patriot."

Toby merely grunted, disgusted at himself for losing a chance at regicide.

After reloading the heavy pistol and tamping down the shot in its long barrel, Paddy now took aim at the turnip in the field. The late afternoon sun was in his eyes and the target seemed to bob up and down before his eyes even as he tried to steady his arm.

"Steady now," said Jordan, encouragingly. "Keep that arm steady."

A second shot rang out in the field, sending more birds scattering into the air, but still, the turnip kept its seat atop the barrels.

The boys were growing frustrated. Neither seemed to have the knack for consistently hitting their targets, and Jordan was worried at the amount of shot they were going through, an expense for which he now was paying from his own pocket. Also, though their nearest neighbours were several miles away, Jordan was concerned that someone would hear the regular shots coming from the Byrne farm and start asking questions.

"Damn it all, Ned!" spat Paddy with frustration, glaring at the pistol. "We practice every day and still miss the damn turnip."

"Your last shot didn't even come close," sneered Toby with satisfaction, fed up with his brother's boasting.

"Yours might as well've hit the barn, you were so far off the mark," retorted Paddy, his temper flaring.

"Calm yourselves, lads," said Jordan, weary of the brothers' constant bickering. He had to admit that neither of the boys seemed very likely to become a proficient marksman—both seemed to have the same poor eyesight which no amount of training could overcome.

While the boys argued over who had come closer to hitting the English king, Jordan sat down on a crumbling stone wall that girded Breckinridge's field and considered his predicament. The boys' father, seeing no future for his sons as tenant farmers, had told Jordan to make fighters of them. This he viewed as an honourable undertaking, although one certainly born of dire circumstances.

Looking up, Jordan saw Paddy tackle his brother and pin him to the ground. Jordan mused that the lad showed a certain skillfulness at wrestling and that he might do better at hand-to-hand combat. Bayonet thrusts were just as deadly as rifle shots, after all, and not every man was born to be a sharpshooter. He would change tactics.

"Come on," he called out to the twins, who continued their struggles on the dry, hard-packed dirt of the field. "Enough shooting for one day. We'll have dinner, then begin a new drill."

"Ah, Ned," said Paddy, dirt-streaked and clearly disappointed. "Can't we shoot some more? We know we aren't great marksmen such as yourself, but we will practice and try to do you proud."

"Not every man was born to fire a gun, Padraig," said Jordan with resignation in his voice. "Every man has a different talent, given to him by the Almighty. It is up to him to find out what that talent is and to put it to good use in this short life."

"If we cannot shoot the King, will you, Ned? It is a shame to see him lording it over us still from his throne," said Toby with a smirk.

"No, lad."

"Do, Ned!" Paddy chimed in. "Show us how it is done."

Jordan shook his head, laughing. "We've wasted enough bullets for one day, lads. Your mother will be happy to see her turnip back again in time for tomorrow's dinner."

"Please, Ned! One shot—or are you afraid you will miss?"

Jordan's patience was wearing thin. "Give me the damn gun, then," he snapped at Paddy, who eagerly handed it over to his teacher. With a quick motion, Jordan tamped the ball and powder down the barrel and raised the weapon to shoulder height. Staring down the barrel of the gun at the target, Jordan caught a flash of his father's pale, round face in the smooth skin of the turnip and pulled the trigger, sending a shower of vegetable pulp raining down into the field. The boys applauded wildly, slapping Jordan on the back and shaking their heads at the ease with which he always seemed to hit his targets. But they also recognized the dark look of concentration that passed over their teacher's face in the moment before the gun was fired, and felt a chill. It was like the sudden black clouds that sometimes swept in from the ocean, obscuring the sun and casting long shadows across the rich greens of the fields below.

"There now," said Jordan with finality. "Let's have no more of your infernal pestering."

The boys raised a cheer as the trio turned their backs to the field and made for home and dinner. "Down with the king! Down with England! Long live Edward Jordan, defender of Ireland!"

Jordan smiled at the twins' enthusiasm and was flattered by their admiration for him. He felt an older brother's kind of protectiveness toward the Byrne boys, whose inexperience with fighting was obvious and troubling in the present circumstance. Jordan reflected that he had earned his share of black eyes and bruised knuckles growing up in Carlow, where huddled gangs of boys seemed to fight each other on a daily basis when they were not throwing rocks at hurlers at the Tobacco Meadows or sneaking into the backs of public houses to watch the cockfights. Ned Jordan did not possess the audacity of some of these small scrappers, although he did spend a good deal of his childhood on the streets of Carlow. He especially dreaded evenings when his father returned from his day's work as a tanner, having stopped at the public house on the way home, and his parents would begin the arguments that invariably resulted in his mother being beaten. Ned could not bear to hear his mother's cries and pleas for mercy, nor his father's angry methodical grunts as he landed blow after blow with the buckle end of his belt on his wife's prone body. Once, when he was five, and when his mother had been pregnant with his sister, Ned had tried to come between his father and mother just as another beating had commenced. His father had kicked him aside like a puppy while his mother had pleaded, "Go to bed now, Neddy. Your Da has had a hard day. Don't bother him now—run along, Neddy boy. Ma will be fine."

With sharp pain from his father's kick still reverberating through his ribs, little Ned had known that his mother was lying to him, and he felt a mixture of sadness, fear and growing anger at her for letting his father use her so. He would never again try to stop his father from hitting his mother; thereafter, as he lay in bed at night listening to her cries, a low chant would begin inside his head that lulled him to sleep, even as the tears streamed down his small face, "She asked for it. She asked for it."

NED DREADED HIS FATHER, Robert Jordan, and feared his anger. It seemed nothing he ever did was good enough for the man. As a sixteen-year-old, having stopped going to school and knowing his father would not care one way or the other, Ned asked Robert if he could be taken on at the tannery, a request he thought would surely please the old man. Instead, Robert spat his gob of tobacco onto the floor with disgust, and cursed his son out for a fool for entertaining such thoughts.

"You want to end your days a penniless, miserable wretch with a bitch of a wife who'll squawk at you every morning and night, wanting more of your money—your health ruined, the bottle your only comfort in this world—you go ahead, my lad. Be a tanner like your Da. You see what a success he is."

Ned was speechless. He ran out of the kitchen where he and Robert had been sitting, not able to get away fast enough from his father's house, from the unhappiness that poisoned it. He wanted to leave Carlow altogether, but where could he go? His family had lived there for generations; they had no relatives and few acquaintances outside the town's confines.

He ran until his legs began to buckle beneath him and he was forced to stop and catch his breath. His swift flight had carried him some distance outside of town along a hard-packed dirt path leading out into the lush green countryside. The hills brooded menacingly off in the distance, fitting companions for young Jordan in his dark mood.

It was growing dark and he had no wish to return home. He spent the night at the side of the road beneath the hedgerows, his thin wool coat wrapped tightly around him, his face pointed toward the sky and its vast geography of stars. Such immense space, and still Ned Jordan felt a claustrophobic despair thinking of his own life. It was clear to him that Robert's bitter retort to a well-meant gesture of solidarity was a turning point: he could no longer continue to live in his father's house, enduring his rages against his wife, children and the world. He felt sure that his departure would mean the end of his relationship with his mother as well, who for all her angry recriminations against her husband would never think of leaving him, nor imagine that one of her children could sever ties with his father.

A chill wind passed over the boy's prone figure, stinging his eyes as they welled up with tears. For the first time in his life, he felt entirely alone, no longer Robert Jordan's boy, but just plain Ned Jordan. He suddenly felt much older than his sixteen years, and very frightened. The voice from every sleepless childhood bedtime spoke to him again, with the same stern timbre it had always had:

"Stop your crying, boy, and be a man! You must make your own way now. If your father pounds your mother to an early grave, that is no longer your concern. It is a cruel world, and you must steel yourself."

The boy fell asleep with the echoes of his father's tirade still painfully fresh.

Awakening the next morning with the dew damp upon him, his limbs stiff and sore, Ned Jordan could not immediately remember where he was. Then the details of the previous day's flight from his father's house came rushing back in a tide, and he was filled with sadness. Mingled with that sadness, though, was a fresh sense of resolve, one that Jordan knew he must act upon. And so he turned his back on the town of his birth and began the long journey to Dublin.

Chapter 2

Jordan found that the road to Dublin from Carlow was a well-frequented one, and he had no dearth of offers of a lift for portions of the trip. As he jostled along in the back of a cheerful farmer's squeaky wagon, Jordan felt his despair dissipating with every mile he put between himself and Carlow. He knew that he had made the right choice and barely gave a thought to how frantic his mother and younger sister would be when they discovered that he had disappeared.

He found work almost immediately upon his arrival in a print shop as printer's devil, and his aptitude for the work soon earned him the confidence of the shop's owner, Tom Brennan, whose son William was a year younger than Jordan. The younger Brennan, a heavyset, taciturn boy, would regularly stop by his father's shop on his way home from school, where he was an indifferent student, like Ned Jordan had been. He was usually eating something; on his first meeting with Jordan, it had been a piece of overcooked mutton that he had pocketed surreptitiously from a hapless schoolmate's lunch-pail earlier that day. Leaning against the table where Jordan had been set to work cleaning type with a dirty rag, Willy Brennan remarked,

"Sure, that's a tedious job my da has you doing."

Jordan shrugged, continuing to polish. "It's better than begging on the street."

Brennan shrugged back, chewing ruminatively on his mutton. "He tried to get me to do some jobs around the shop once, said he'd pay me a shilling for every day's work I put in. I lasted one afternoon."

Jordan looked incredulous. That was more than he made working for old man Brennan.

He kept silent, but could not contain a look of disgust at the sight of the plump and greasy-faced lad munching noisily in front of him.

The younger Brennan continued, oblivious to Jordan's resentment. "Who needs filthy work like this when there's real money to be made in land speculation in America? That's where I aim to go, soon as my Ma'll let me out of her sight and my father gives up on the idea of having me take over his business."

It seemed obvious to Jordan that Willy Brennan was far too lazy and self-important to make anything of himself, either in Ireland or America, but again, he kept these thoughts to himself.

Willy spoke again. "You don't say much, do you? Da said you was a brooding sort. Didn't tell him much about what sort of people you come from. He said the only thing you would say for certain was that you came from Carlow."

"That's right," said Jordan warily.

"My mother's people come from there," said Willy nonchalantly as he gave his mutton bone one last scouring with his teeth before tossing it into a corner. He licked his fingers with deliberate care and wiped them dry on the seat of his greasy trousers. "Most of the ones with any brains have sailed for the Boston states. An uncle of mine runs a linen business that caters to the fine ladies of New Amsterdam. Sails the stuff over from here and can charge what he likes for the stuff they wouldn't thank you for in London. He wrote Ma that I'm welcome to join him whenever she thinks best—there's more than enough business. That's where I'll be living in a few years' time, in New York. To hell with the old man and his dirty little shop."

The young man's complacency bewildered Jordan, to whom such insolence would have spelled an immediate beating or worse from his father. He would never have dreamed of speaking of his family in such a way, especially to a complete stranger. He had a strong desire to tell the plump young man what he thought of him, but could not afford to lose his job at Brennan's shop. Instead, he said, "Pardon me, but I must be at my work." He lowered his head and returned to polishing.

"Suit yourself then," said Willy, and stood idly for a few moments watching Jordan work. Realizing he would get no more out of his father's new employee, he turned and walked out of the shop, whistling a tune.

Over the following months, it became obvious to Jordan that Willy Brennan visited the shop he professed to despise so much because he had no friends and little to occupy his time. He talked almost incessantly to Jordan, revealing that he had stopped going to school, though he kept the fact well-concealed from his father and continued to appear at the shop at the same hour every afternoon at the conclusion of the school day. One sunny afternoon in late spring, he coaxed Jordan to leave his work and accompany him on a short jaunt around the neighbourhood.

"I'll get Da to find you an errand, then we'll have some larks."

Though he had no particular desire to spend time in the company of the younger Brennan, Jordan was eager to leave the confines of the dark shop for a time and was glad when Mr. Brennan entrusted him with the delivery of some freshly printed handbills to the local theatre.

Setting out from the print shop at a brisk pace, the two boys soon arrived at the dingy red brick building that housed the Sons of Erin Players, a small troupe of struggling actors who had their handbills printed at Brennan's, usually on credit that they were a long time in paying. Willy's father, sympathetic to the plight of the thespian, rarely pressed the group for money owed; instead, the

Sons of Erin often invited Tom Brennan and his family to their performances, which occasionally featured a kindly business owner whose personality was remarkably like Brennan's.

Ned and Willy entered the building by the side alley where deliveries were made and heavy stage props unloaded. The interior of the building was dark and cavernous, with the damp and musty smell Jordan associated with a church manse. Heavy velvet curtains hung on either side of a dilapidated stage; from the dim light of an upper window, Jordan could see that the curtains were old and threadbare and that the plaster moldings around the ceiling were cracked and falling down. There was a sadness about the theatre that spoke of past glories that would never return; Jordan did not care to linger long in such a building.

Brennan led the way through the treacherous backstage area where heavy set pieces, furniture and props were left carelessly lying about, serving as a booby trap to the uninitiated. He seemed at home among the clutter, and surprisingly agile picking his way through it, as though he had done so many times before. Jordan tripped over a rickety chaise longue, banging his shins and spilling his sack of handbills onto the floor. He cursed loudly, his temper flaring. "Just where in Jesus' name are we going?" he asked Willy loudly, his voice echoing in the cavernous space. Brennan bent to help Jordan gather up the bills and stuff them back into his sack, the first real work Jordan had ever seen him do. "It's this way," he said, gesturing vaguely in the gloom.

"The boys rehearse in a room out back to save lighting the theatre. I've been here before," he said with a knowing look.

The boys found the Sons of Erin in a room the size of a closet with no windows tucked far in the back of the building. The air was thick with tobacco smoke and Jordan found himself struggling for breath as they entered the room where the eleven actors were gathered.

"Good day, lads," said a red-faced man in a dirty shirt as Jordan set the handbills on the table where the men appeared to be in the middle of a game of cards. "You must be the new lad from Brennan's. How are ye today, Willy?"

Brennan nodded. "Fine, and yourself?"

"Never better. You lads care to join us for a round of whist?"

"Sure, and why not?" said Willy, motioning to Jordan to join him at the cramped card table.

Jordan was reluctant—he had no desire to stay in the smoky room any longer than was necessary. "Ah, Willy," he said in a low voice. "Your father'll be expecting me before long. We should go."

"For God's sake, Ned, are you afraid of the old man? Leave him to me," said Brennan with a smirk. "Deal us in, Mick," he said to the red-faced man. "My friend here is from the country and don't know his manners yet."

Embarrassed, Jordan sat down, his eyes watering from the smoke. He wasn't long in coming to the conclusion that the Sons of Erin seemed more interested in politics than in theatre, or cards, for that matter. They had barely finished the first round of whist before someone mentioned "that great republic across the Atlantic," and the situation in France. Knowing looks were exchanged among the players as the talk inevitably turned to Irish politics. Jordan himself had never cared particularly whether Ireland was ruled by the king of England or the pope in Rome, but the Sons of Erin seemed to care a very great deal about such things.

"Why is it the Yankee Doodle dandies have got themselves a declaration that says all men are created equal with the right to bear arms, and the Irish people that have lived on this land for hundreds of years have never come close to doing the same?"

"They hate the British same as we do; they're our friends, sure. What's to say we can't join with our friends and throw the bastards out?"

"'Tis coming, boys, 'tis coming. I feel it in the marrow of me bones. Ireland will belong to the Irish before my life is over, you mark my words."

Jordan felt very uncomfortable listening to this kind of talk, which he felt sure could only lead to trouble. He distrusted these men, who seemed nothing more than braggarts and layabouts who refused real work. He looked over at Brennan to gauge his reaction. In place of Willy's usual bored and sulky demeanor was an expression of earnest attentiveness that made Jordan very uneasy. He stood up abruptly.

"I must be getting back to my work now," he said, his words sounding awkward in his ears.

"What's your hurry, lad?" asked one of the actors, blowing out a lazy stream of pipe smoke as he spoke. "Old man Brennan knows you're with us—he's sympathetic to our cause, just like his good son William here." Willy nodded, proudly.

"And what cause would that be?" Jordan asked, unable to restrain the note of contempt in his voice.

"We're part of the brotherhood," said the red-faced man while his fellows nodded sagely.

"Willy's joined us and you could too, lad."

Jordan looked at Willy incredulously. "You've decided to become an actor?"

Laughter erupted at the card table. Willy spoke condescendingly to the bewildered Jordan. "You mean to say you've truly never heard of the brotherhood? The United Irishmen?"

"No. Should I have?"

"Indeed you should, if you believe Ireland deserves her independence from England."

Jordan looked disbelieving. "Is that what you're hoping for? That the English will leave Ireland? Well then, you might as well wish that the ocean were full of whisky instead of salt water for all the good it'll do."

Willy spoke up with uncharacteristic fervour. "You're wrong, Ned. If a few thousand men in the colonies can repulse an English army and navy, what's to stop the Irish from doing the same?"

"How old are you now, lad?" asked the red-faced man of Jordan, laying his arm around his thin shoulder and leering at him.

"I'll be nineteen this May."

"We have young bucks of twelve and thirteen joining our number across the country. You'd make a fine soldier in an Irish army, my boy."

"I have no desire to die from an English bullet. I wish only to make my way in the world and leave politics to the lords in Westminster and Dublin Castle. Good day." With that, Jordan turned quickly on his heel and exited the claustrophobia of the small room. He could hear Willy's sneering voice calling after him, "We'll see you back within the fortnight, Ned Jordan!"

For weeks following his brief encounter with the Sons of Erin, Jordan had the uneasy feeling that he was being watched. It could have been young Brennan's newly menacing presence at the shop, as though challenging Jordan to speak of what he had heard at the theatre, whose patrons believed that the Sons of Erin were merely rehearsing plays, not fomenting rebellion. Jordan was nervous in Mr. Brennan's presence now, too. The old man had chastised him for his late return from the theatre, asking him what had taken him so long. Jordan had not known what to say, unsure how sympathetic Brennan truly was to the Sons of Erin's secret cause and not wanting to be known as a tattler.

On the streets of certain quarters of the city, an air of quiet conspiracy was brewing. Members of the brotherhood now often travelled with prayer books hidden in their pockets in order to swear in new members. Increasingly, Jordan felt left out of the excitement as young men of his acquaintances left their lodgings in the evenings to attend secret meetings whose locations they never divulged to the uninitiated. It seemed every young man Jordan's age now belonged to the brotherhood. When asked about what went on at their meetings, his friends would only wink and ask the secret-handshake question that seemed to be on everyone's lips these days: "Are you Up?"

Finally, Jordan took Willy Brennan aside one day after work and asked when the next general meeting of the brotherhood was to be held.

"And what would you be wanting to know that for?" asked Willy nonchalantly, though visibly pleased.

"It seems a man can't get work done anymore without being pestered every minute about when he'll join the damned brotherhood. Since I can't get any peace, I might as well join and see what all the fuss is about." In fact, none of Jordan's acquaintances had ever mentioned his joining the society; it was his own feeling of being left out that had finally and convinced him to approach Brennan.

"Did I not tell you you'd join us some day soon, lad?"

"Never mind that. When do you next meet?"

Brennan hesitated a moment, then, judging his friend to be in earnest, said, "Thursday next at the theatre. A dozen new recruits are to be sworn in and begin training."

"Training for what?" asked Jordan, though he already knew the answer.

"You know what for, Jordan," said Brennan, smirking. "The English won't simply up and leave if we ask them politely. There'll be fighting to be done, and we need training."

"And who will teach us how to fight and provide us with the weapons?" asked Jordan, almost rhetorically. "You well know the British have the only regular army in Ireland—does the brotherhood expect to storm their arsenals and seize their muskets and cannon right out from under their noses?"

Brennan looked uncomfortable. "Sure—no one is claiming it'll be easy, Ned. But don't discount the French. They've gotten rid of their own king and may help us get rid of the one that enslaves us, sitting over there in London."

"What makes you think the French would risk their own hides to help a foreign country?"

"You ask too many questions."

"You haven't answered me."

Brennan shrugged. "We're all Catholics in the UI; we look after our own."

"Fitzgerald's a Protestant—so are Morris and Johnson and at least five others I can think of. I thought the brotherhood was for all Irishmen, regardless of their religion or profession."

"And how might you be knowing so much about the brotherhood, Ned Jordan?" asked Brennan, sulkily.

"I hear things around the shop," shrugged Jordan. "You might too, if you ever stopped eating long enough to listen."

Brennan's face reddened, and his meaty fist shot out impulsively at Jordan's face. Ducking the blow, Jordan rammed his head into Brennan's round stomach, sending him pitching backwards on the ground where he lay moaning for several minutes before staggering to his feet.

Jordan stood nearby, his arms crossed.

"What foolishness is this, Brennan?" he said, mockingly. "Perhaps you're not the man to lead the training for the brotherhood."

Brennan spat at Jordan. "Son of a whore…Da will be hearing of this…"

Swiftly, Jordan collared Brennan, his eyes like hot coals burning in their sockets. "One word and I'll serve you ten times worse than just now. You'll wish you were never born. Do you mark me?"

Brennan nodded, his face pale.

He had learned never to begin an argument with Ned Jordan.

Chapter 3

May 25, 1798, Carlow, Ireland—

They marched on Carlow before dawn on a soft spring day, twelve hundred United Irishmen. They marched in silence, a ragged line of green-capped rebels, so far unopposed, fear growing in their stomachs. Where were the government soldiers? It was too quiet, too easy. Their homemade pikes and clubs rested uneasily on their shoulders. No rifles had come from France in the end, the small French fleet having been scattered in a Christmas Eve storm in Bantry Bay. Most of the twelve hundred men were not yet aware of the capture of their leaders, Wolfe Tone and Edward Fitzgerald, and of the long, agonized deaths that awaited them—one from a slow-acting English bullet, one from a shaky, suicidal hand.

Just at the entrance to the town, a wave of uncertainty seemed to pass over the men and they halted, unwilling to proceed. Mick Heydon stepped forward, saying, "I will go into the potato-market alone and ask if the people are ready to join us, as we agreed. If they are not, we will not ask you to advance even a step further."

There was much heated murmuring among the men following Heydon's departure and a new fear, sharper than any Ned Jordan had ever experienced, took hold—the fear bred in the agonizing moments waiting for a battle to begin. Some of the men had the impulse to drop their pikes and run, but were prevented from doing so by their leaders, a few of whom carried blunderbusses and threatened to blow out the brains of any man who deserted or disheartened his fellows.

The minutes crept by, and the sky began to lighten. Soon, Heydon's familiar shape was spotted hurrying back to the company of rebels, urging them, "March on! The people are with us; victory is ours, boys!" There was nothing for it now—despite Heydon's brave words, Jordan knew their fates were now sealed.

A few sympathetic Carlow townsfolk came out of their houses onto the cobbled streets to welcome them, old men slapping their backs, women throwing their arms around their necks, kissing them, stroking their hair. Little children surrounded the men, clutching their mothers' skirts, lisping "God bless you, boys—God bless Ireland."

Ned Jordan had not been back to Carlow in over a decade, and reflected now on the strangeness of this homecoming. He had long ago lost whatever sense of idealism he had possessed in relation to the brotherhood, though he had often paid it lip service when in the company of his fellows, the Byrnes especially, who expected nothing less than fervent patriotism from him. Why had he lied to them, to himself, about his motives? He had joined the brotherhood for companionship—why did he now feel so utterly alone?

He hoped that the townsfolk who came out to greet the marchers would not recognize him in the early dawn light, though he recognized many of them from his childhood. He had grown much taller, of course, and during his time at the Byrnes' had grown a thick black beard. Though life in the city had matured him, coming back to Carlow gave him the same feeling of dread he had experienced as a child helplessly listening to his mother being beaten. He did not know if either of his parents still lived, and the greater part of him did not wish to know. Now, marching alongside the foolish Willy Brennan and the other rebels, their green caps set at rakish angles on their heads, armed only with sticks against the companies of Yeomen's Militia and Ninth Dragoons he knew were waiting for them, Jordan felt like a thief about to be caught red-handed.

As the rebels approached the potato market, their appointed meeting place with the townsmen Heydon had spoken to just a short while earlier, Jordan felt an eerie calm. They passed the closed shopfronts and shuttered windows of the houses—where were their friends? No one awaited them except the snipers from the garrison who had been waiting in upper rooms all night and now sent a hail of bullets into the street below. Panic—this kind of ambush could not be countered except with guns—rebels dropping their useless pikes and staves and running for their lives—more armed soldiers waiting for them on the ground, running after them—breaking through houses, sheds and cabins where women and children screamed with fright and were trampled upon—outside, more soldiers setting alight houses where some rebels had taken refuge. Jordan ran, ran for his life—turning down the narrow Bridewell Lane, now a shooting gallery for the English, he felt the rush of air from passing bullets graze his clothes and ruffle his hair. Around him, acrid smoke filled the air as two hundred civilians burned to death in their homes. In his panicked dash for shelter on Tullow Street, Jordan saw Paddy Byrne running full speed into a burning house where the screams of children could be heard through the chaos; he thought later that that had been the cleanest way to die that day. Like many of the unarmed Irishmen, Willy Brennan had been shot in the throat and bled to death on the cobbles of Moidart Street. Toby Byrne had simply disappeared. Altogether, five hundred rebels and townsfolk had been killed that morning; not a single English soldier had died.

Exhausted, wheezing from the smoke and dazed from the horrors he had witnessed, Jordan had finally collapsed on the roadside, quite near the place he had once slept the night he ran away from home. He shivered convulsively. His green cap gave him away to the English officer who was riding by on his way to reinforce the garrison, and he was led away in chains.

JORDAN'S INCARCERATION in the Carlow gaol prevented him from witnessing the horrific reprisals that continued for ten days—the hangings, bludgeonings, shootings and disembowellings of one hundred and fifty Irish men and women for their part in the ill-starred rebellion. Jordan did not know why he was being spared a summary execution for his role in the rebellion, and when, two weeks later, he was brought out of his cell and transported to the courthouse, he still half-expected to meet a firing squad rather than a town magistrate for a preliminary examination. He stared at his feet while his accuser spoke, barely hearing him.

"Edward Jordan, you are being tried on charges of sedition and high treason for the crime of membership in the Society of United Irishmen. In addition, we have been informed that for a period of two months, you were engaged in the arming and training of men for the purpose of fomenting a rebellion in the town of Carlow. Is this the case?" asked the magistrate.

"Yes, sir. I do not deny that I trained 'em."

"So you plead guilty to the charges being brought against you?"

Jordan hesitated for a moment. Then he said, "Yes, I am guilty."

"Let it be recorded that the prisoner has entered a plea of 'guilty'" said the magistrate in a bored voice. He had seen a stream of men like Edward Jordan pass through his chambers all day and for much of the previous week; the sooner they passed through the bowels of the system and were hanged, the better. The gaols were already bulging at the seams with scum like Ned Jordan, and the sham of attempting due process in a clear case of sedition seemed to him a gross waste of time and effort. If this had been the Royal Navy, Jordan would have been flogged to death. The magistrate sighed. He would never be through with them, that much was plain. On the table in front of him was a small pile of death warrants requiring his signature. He removed one from the top of the heap and cursorily signed his name as he spoke. "The prisoner Ned Jordan is remanded to prison to await trial at the earliest opportunity." He dismissed Jordan with an impatient wave of the hand.

"Warden! Bring the next prisoner."

JORDAN'S NEXT VISIT to the magistrate was after his sentencing. He listened in silence as his crimes were read back to him, along with the punishment befitting them, in the view of His Majesty's loyal representative: death.

"Have you anything to say, prisoner Jordan?" asked the magistrate as he signed the order for execution.

"No, sir, I have not," replied Jordan.

Putting down his pen, the magistrate peered with sudden interest at the prisoner standing before him over the rim of his glasses.

"They say you were training men to fight, Jordan. How many of 'em were there?"

"Beg your pardon, sir?"

"Come, come, man. How many men did you train?" snapped the magistrate with scorn.

Jordan hesitated for a moment. "Two, sir. They were just boys."

"And what are the names of these boys?"

"Beg your pardon again, sir, but I ain't an informer. They're likely dead now anyway, God rest their souls."

The magistrate removed his spectacles and gnawed on one end of them.

"You may be interested to know, Mr. Jordan, that His Majesty is offering His gracious pardon to any man who will give the names of those participating in the late rebellion. As an 'officer' of the brotherhood, you know the names of many of the rebels who are still at large. We will not let such men go unpunished. You can spare yourself punishment by giving us the names of these men. Your brotherhood is broken; Tone has slit his own throat in an English prison— he saw how much you can trust the French. As for you, Jordan, your fate lies entirely in your own hands. Will you help us?"

Jordan hesitated for several moments. He was being asked to betray the most sacred precept of the brotherhood: loyalty. He had sworn to maintain this loyalty even unto death. But what did all that matter now? The brotherhood had unravelled—their leaders were either dead or dying now. Should he also die for a cause that was already lost?

With a deathly pallor in his face, Jordan began a mechanical recitation. "Sean O'Driscoll and Joe Collins are engaged in smuggling guns into Wexford—they are the only ones of any importance that I know about from this area. You have killed or imprisoned the rest."

The magistrate nodded, jotting down the names in a notebook.

"Mr. O'Driscoll I know well, but Collins I have not met. Where would I go to pay him a call?"

Jordan spoke through clenched teeth: "The last I heard, he was living on the Kilcullen Road in Wexford."

"Thank you, Mr. Jordan," he smiled, picking up Jordan's execution order and tearing it into pieces. "You have been of immense help. Warden—show Mr. Jordan out and make sure he has all his belongings with him when he leaves."

Stumbling out of the dark gaol into the bright June sunlight, his small bundle of clothing clutched against his chest, Ned Jordan had trouble believing that he was once again a free man. He gazed about him at the burned shops and houses of the town of his unhappy childhood. Ireland would never belong to the Irish—this much had been made clear to him and the other survivors of the rebellion. England's iron fist had once again pummeled its colony into servility. Mixed with the bitterness of defeat felt by many of his countrymen was a new and far more personal anguish for Jordan: his betrayal of two sworn brethren of the United Irishmen. He had not known O'Driscoll personally, but Collins was an old acquaintance, and when the rebels were finally defeated at Wexford in early October, both men were rounded up and quickly executed.

Seized with the same impulse to flee as he had felt a decade before, for the second time in his life, Jordan ran out of Carlow and did not look back.

JORDAN COULD HARDLY ACCOUNT for his life in the five years following the rebellion, those desperate, furtive years he lived in dread of being discovered as a traitor, his bad conscience gnawing steadily at his soul. He returned to Dublin, hoping that Mr. Brennan would give him back his job at the print shop, but the old man wanted nothing more to do with him since his son's death. Jordan felt the sharp cut of Brennan's resentment, his obvious wish that it had been Jordan killed and not Willy, an unfairness that rankled with him. He began to fear being seen in broad daylight on the streets of Dublin, and avoided walking in the main streets except around dawn and dusk, when he fancied the indistinct light made him less recognizable.

With Dublin and its unhappy memories making his life nearly intolerable, Jordan moved to Cork and settled under a new name, hoping not to be recognized by his former associates. He took many jobs—shopkeeper's clerk, fisherman, street-sweeper—and barely made enough money to eat. He met Margaret McMorran, the daughter of a fish monger to whom he sometimes sold his catch, and fell in love with her dark beauty. Her prospects were poor enough that her father allowed the match, though he never liked Jordan. It was not long after their marriage and the arrival of their first child, a boy named Edward, that Jordan began once more to be visited regularly by the nightmare that had plagued him in the days before the rebellion. The vision was so disturbing, it sometimes kept him from returning to sleep. He lived in a state of constant anxiety of being discovered, and even the slightest provocation could ignite his anger. Margaret had to tiptoe around the house and hush the baby's crying when her husband returned home in the evenings—she quickly learned to fear Ned Jordan's short-fuse temper and the violence that often resulted from it.

It was at twilight one evening as Jordan was walking home from a wearying day sweeping the streets of Cork and reflecting on the utter futility of trying to keep any road in a port city free from garbage that he was accosted by two men he had never seen before.

"Jordan, you son of a whore," said one man with a scar running down his cheek as he seized Jordan's left wrist. The other man stepped in toward him and pressed a knife against his chest. They propelled him into an alley off the main thoroughfare where the stink of rotten vegetables and human excrement was overpowering. The scarred assailant spoke again.

"Joe and me, we was friends of Sean O'Driscoll, and we don't like it that you're still alive while he's rotting in his grave. Do we, Joe?"

The second man shook his head, pressing the knife closer into Jordan's chest, slicing into flesh.

"We know 'twas you betrayed him and we've come to serve you as you served him and Collins. Ain't we, Joe?"

The man nodded again. Jordan felt blood soaking into his sweaty shirt. He thought he would faint.

"You've got the wrong man," he said in a faltering voice, unconvincing even to himself, while the men bore in on him, their foul breath mingling with the nauseating alley air.

"My name is Jim O'Carroll and I have a wife and son at home."

The men laughed. "That you do, Mr. Jordan. We'll be paying them a visit this day and will be sure to tell your widow to say a few Hail Marys over your body. That is, if we don't kill her first."

Jordan felt a rush of furious energy electrify his whole body, and with a sudden twisting motion, broke free from the grasp of his attacker, driving his knee hard into the groin of the man holding the knife, who doubled over with an unearthly groan, sending the knife clattering to the cobbles below. Jordan now ran with a speed he did not know he possessed, ducking through alleys and vaulting fences, and soon outdistanced his would-be killers.

Bolting through his kitchen door, breathless and blood-soaked, he grabbed Margaret by the wrist and shoved her into the back room.

"Quick!" he Gaspéd. "Pack our things, woman. They've found me at last—we must leave this place at once."

Bewildered, Margaret stared at her husband as he tried to staunch the flow of blood from his chest with a dirty towel.

"Ned, what happened? Who did this to you?"

"Do as I say!" Jordan yelled, waking the baby, who began to howl. "There's no time to explain. We take the first ship to leave Cork."

Tears streaming down her cheeks, Margaret began throwing their few possessions into a sheet she pulled from the bed; they did not own a trunk. She tucked the baby underneath her thin coat and muffled its cries against her chest. Jordan grabbed from the mantelpiece the bottle that contained all the money they had in the world: barely two days' wages. How would they get away from this place with no money?

They hurried to the dockyard from where the ships left for the new world, Jordan checking over his shoulder at every step. They slept that night between two huge coils of rope, a blanket thrown over their heads to hide them. Neither Jordan nor Margaret slept. Early the next morning, leaving Margaret and the baby shivering beneath the blanket, Jordan paced along the wharves, scanning for a ship that looked as if it were preparing for imminent departure. He noticed a group of stevedores hoisting a number of heavy crates on pulleys onto a capacious-looking barque whose nameplate read *Penelope*. From her size and the volume of cargo being loaded, Jordan wagered she was bound for some place across the Atlantic, exactly where he wanted to be. The precise location did not matter.

Keeping a safe distance from the loading activities aboard *Penelope*, Jordan waited and watched as the last of the crates was hauled up and placed safely on deck. He could see that the crates would remain on deck—the ship was riding low in the water, a sure sign that the hold was already full. She now awaited only her complement of human cargo.

Their work completed, the stevedores dispersed, leaving the wharf empty. Jordan could see the morning watch strolling somewhat sleepily along the port side of the vessel, gazing blankly at the crates. If they could just make it past him and onto the ship, they might be able to keep hidden among the cargo until the ship was well on its journey.

Oblivious that he was being watched, and much to Jordan's delight, the watchman gave a quick glance over each shoulder, and quickly passed down the companionway steps to ask the cook for a second piece of bread—he reckoned he could do this in less than three minutes at this early hour and no one but the trusty cook would be any the wiser. Seizing a blessed opportunity, Jordan sprinted for the hiding place where he had left his little family, and hauling Margaret to her feet and hissing at her to shut the baby up, propelled them up *Penelope*'s unprotected gangway and behind a pile of crates into a space barely large enough to accommodate two adults. They hardly dared breathe, listening for the sound of the watchman's footsteps coming back up the companionway, praying that the baby would not give them away.

The watchman returned several minutes later, brushing bread crumbs off his beard and looking well satisfied. He strolled slowly past the Jordans' hiding place several times, humming "Sweet Molly Malone." Jordan felt a cold sweat beading on the back of his neck. What would happen if they were discovered? He dared not pursue the thought further.

"Good day to you!" called the friendly voice of a curious onlooker from the wharf below to the watchman, whose back Jordan could just see as he leaned over the port rail. He could not see the speaker.

"And to you," the watchman called back.

"A fair wind today—and it looks like she's fully loaded. When do you sail?"

"We've a dozen passengers to board—I expect them within the hour."

"She's a fine-looking ship, sir."

The watch nodded casually. "That she is. She's been three times to New York and acquitted herself nobly each time. I expect the same from her this trip, God willing."

Jordan and Margaret exchanged a silent look as they absorbed these pieces of eavesdropped information.

"Well, fair winds and a safe journey to you and *Penelope*," said the onlooker, tipping his hat to the watch and strolling away.

It wasn't long before the Jordans heard the bustle of dockside activity as a group of passengers prepared to board the ship. The creak and groan of the gangway as heavy trunks were carried aboard mingled with the sounds of tearful voices bidding farewell to their loved ones and wishing them God's blessings in their new life across the ocean. Jordan felt a sharp pang in his chest; no one stood on the wharf to wish him and his little family farewell. He looked over and saw the tears running down Margaret's cheeks. He wanted to reach across and comfort her, but dared not make even the smallest movement until they were safely embarked.

They heard the rapid footsteps of the deckhands as they prepared to make sail and raise anchor, accompanied by the barked orders of the mate. As the ship glided away from the wharf and made for the open water, Jordan experienced the first twinges of something he had hardly felt before and did not immediately recognize: relief. Since the rebellion, each day had felt like a kind of slow-motion steeplechase in which he was being relentlessly pursued, knowing even one misstep could spell disaster. Now, with Ireland and his pursuers at his back, perhaps he could leave his unhappy past behind him and hope for better things in the future. He smiled at Margaret, who looked startled—in more than a year of marriage, she had seen her husband smile only once or twice. She looked uncomfortable and sad, wedged into the small space behind the packing crates, the baby pressed to her chest. Jordan promised himself that when they got to America, he would be a better husband and father. For now, he dared not allow his little family to come out from their hiding place until the Irish coastline was well behind them.

It was a fine day and the passengers remained above decks for the greater part of it, enjoying the crisp breeze and the still-fresh excitement of sea travel. After the noonday meal of pease porridge and rye bread, one old man lit his pipe and sat smoking contentedly sitting atop the capstan, while three of the younger passengers played hide and seek, ducking in and out among the crates with ease.

Jordan felt the old dread of being discovered come flooding back as a little girl with stringy red hair poked her head around the crate he was crouching behind and addressed him matter-of-factly.

"Sir, you've taken my hiding spot. 'Tis not fair—I'm telling Mam." She turned and ran away.

Jordan made a grab for the tiny girl, but she was so skinny she seemed to slip through his fingers.

He spoke aloud to Margaret for the first time in hours: "We'd best come out now—the jig is up."

Blinking dazedly in the bright sunshine, and clutching their meagre bundle of possessions tightly, the Jordans soon found themselves facing a stern trio of ship's officers.

"What's this, then?" asked the first mate gruffly, looking at the Jordan family as if they were disagreeable insects whose rock he had just upturned. "Stowaways, is it? Trash like you belongs over the side with the kitchen scraps, in my view."

Margaret and the baby began to cry.

The mate continued. "But I'm not the master—he'll decide what's to be done with ye. Come along."

He gave Jordan a shove towards the companionway where the captain was just emerging, having just been told of *Penelope*'s unwanted passengers.

"Well, well, what have we here?" he asked in a brusque tone.

Jordan lowered his head in shame, as a crowd of passengers and crew gathered around his family, staring with reproach. He spoke in a low voice.

"Please you, sir. My wife and I have no money—if we stay in Ireland, it's the debtors' prison for us both and our poor boy will go to the orphanage." He refrained from mentioning the altercation of the day before with the friends of O'Driscoll. "I know I will find work in New York, among my people. I only need to get there."

The captain stroked his salt and pepper beard thoughtfully. He had a kind heart and felt pity for the man who stood pleading before him. He knew he could have Jordan arrested once they arrived in New York, but he felt no desire to add to the family's misery, which was apparent on both Jordans' faces.

He spoke with deliberateness. "I do not consider you a passenger on board this ship for you have not paid your fare—I expect you to perform the duties of a deckhand and earn your keep in that way. Bowen will see to it that you fulfill those duties."

The captain gestured toward the first mate, whose face was twisted into a grimace, evidently none too pleased at the recent turn of events.

Jordan, on the contrary, felt immensely relieved. If he performed well, the captain would presumably not feel it necessary to report him once they reached land.

"Sir—you will find me a willing and capable seaman. I have been to sea—I was a fisherman."

The captain nodded, then turned to the mate.

"See to the necessaries, Bowen. I will take my dinner in a few moments; you may join me when you are free."

Turning back to his new sailor he asked, "What is your name?"

Jordan hesitated for a moment: should he reveal his true identity or continue the charade of being Ned O'Carroll? He looked over at Margaret, a warning in his eyes, as he said,

"Edward Jordan at your service, sir."

His wife looked appalled: wasn't she Margaret O'Carroll? Who was this man she had married?

"Jordan..." A glimmer of recognition passed over the captain's face.

"There were Jordans in Carlow, if I'm not mistaken—were they your people?"

A chill gripped Jordan in the chest as he lied, "No—I have few relations left living, and most of those are in Dublin or Cork."

The captain shrugged.

"Could have sworn I heard Carlow in your voice; my wife's people came from there. The Jordans she knew were a drinking, brawling lot—too fond of beating their wives. I trust you do not fit that description."

Jordan flushed. "No sir—my ma brought me up meek as a lamb."

The captain looked somewhat incredulous.

"I'll have no fighters nor any damn rebels aboard this ship. I hope you will remember that, Mr. Jordan."

With that, the captain dropped easily down the companionway to supper, leaving Jordan wondering how much his new master really knew about his past.

Chapter 4

April 1803, Barque Penelope—

The voyage to New York City was long and uncomfortable, hampered by several storms that left the passengers praying for deliverance. Jordan's sailing experience did not extend to transatlantic crossings nor to large ships, and he fumbled his way through his first week as a deckhand. Though the work was sometimes brutally hard, and Bowen was never the most patient of taskmasters, Jordan took pride in his increasing seamanship as the ship creaked and rolled her way across the unsettled Atlantic. He loved the freedom of the open ocean, the thrill of pitting his own strength against the raw elements. What a great adventure it would be to own such a barque and to ship goods around the world in her! Jordan could envisage such a life for himself: Captain Edward Jordan had a very pleasant sound to his ears.

On the morning that land was sighted by the boatswain, all the passengers crowded at the bow for their first glimpse of the island city of New York. Jordan and three of the other deckhands had been put to work scouring the decks with holystone and paused in their labours for only a moment or two, fearing Bowen's wrath.

Margaret ran over to her husband and embraced him. "We're

here, Ned," she said with emotion in her voice, clutching his arm tightly. "May the good Lord be praised." Suddenly, her expression changed to one of suspicion. "You don't have any other surprises for me, do you?"

Jordan shook his head. He had never told Margaret about his involvement in the rebellion, of course; there were some things about her husband's past that a woman had no need to know.

Jordan grew pale as he watched the distant shape of the land before them slowly grow more distinct. His mind whirled and he felt his old anxiety returning in a rush—what would he and his family do once they arrived? He found himself wishing their journey were not at an end, that he could sail on *Penelope* forever with someone else making the decisions and giving out the orders. He truly enjoyed life at sea. Now, in just a few hours, he would have to start his life over again—not just his own life, but the lives of his wife and son too.

Margaret clearly did not share his husband's apprehension. She had minded the long days at sea, suffering from seasickness and from the looks of contempt she regularly received from the crew and the other passengers. She could not wait to escape the confines of the ship and put her feet back on dry land.

When the ship finally glided into its berth at the Lower Manhattan dockyard late in the afternoon, Margaret was the first passenger to hurry down the gangway, the baby clutched to her breast.

Jordan lingered behind, bidding farewell to his fellow crew mates, and watched enviously as they received their wages from the first mate. There was nothing for it then but to leave the ship and join his family.

THE JORDANS WERE STARTLED by the mixture of accents they heard around them on the waterfront, where swirls of German, Dutch, Italian, and Yiddish seemed to blend in their ears in a fog of incomprehension. Everyone seemed to move and talk at great speed, as though they were late for an important engagement. What seemed like hundreds of horses and wagons clattered by on muddy cobblestones carrying bales of raw cotton, building materials, and barrels of grain and molasses, while pedestrians darted furtively between them, seemingly in all directions. Ned and Margaret were relieved to pick out the Irish accents in the crowd, and in standing still and dazed amid the hubbub that surrounded them, they soon drew the sympathetic attention of a middle-aged passerby, whose black hair and pale skin identified him as a fellow Irishman. He wore a brown tweed overcoat and new shoes, and had a general look of prosperity about him.

"Good day to you!" he said cheerily, tipping his hat to the Jordans. "You have the look of folks who've just come off the boat from the dear old country and think you've entered a madhouse. 'Twas only a few short years ago I was standing just where you are now in much the same predicament." He extended his hand to Jordan. "Name of Harry Farrell."

"I'm Ned Jordan."

The name still had a strange ring to Margaret's ears.

"Very pleased to make your acquaintance, Mr. Jordan. And this must be your fair wife? Mrs. Jordan, I am delighted." He grasped Margaret's hand chivalrously and kissed it lightly. She blushed. Jordan frowned slightly, crossing his arms in front of him. He did not like men paying his wife undue attentions, and spoke rather curtly to the stranger.

"Mr. Farrell, I'd be much obliged if you could direct us to some lodgings for the night."

"I could indeed, my dear sir," said Farrell smoothly, "But then, I would lose the opportunity of having you and your charming wife as my guests for dinner." He looked expectantly at Jordan, then at Margaret, who blushed again.

Jordan felt uneasy, distrusting the stranger's generosity. "That is kind of you, sir—too kind. As you say, we have only just arrived in the city and could not hope to return your generosity to us."

Farrell snorted. "Nonsense, my good man! You can repay me with news from home—sweet Jesus, how I miss it! It will do my heart good to spend the evening in the company of my countrymen." He picked up the small bundle of clothes at the Jordans' feet and began walking briskly towards a row of red brick buildings nearby, leaving the couple little choice but to trot after him.

He entered one of the smaller of the buildings with a small iron schooner hanging over its front door; the first public house Jordan had entered for months. He never had any money left over from his wages for drinking once room and board were paid. Glancing over his shoulder, Farrell winked at Margaret. "The Schooner has the best steak and kidney pie you'll ever encounter this side of paradise." Margaret smiled as she breathed in the rich aromas inside the tavern: sweet pipe tobacco, warm beer and the smell of meat being cooked. Jordan's own mouth began to water as Farrell propelled them toward a table covered by a dirty linen cloth, with empty pewter mugs sitting upon it. Margaret felt the eyes of the male patrons of the tavern upon her and felt self-conscious, especially with the baby asleep in her arms.

"'Tis my table," said Farrell, seating himself comfortably in a rickety chair and gesturing to his guests to do the same. "I like to watch the comings and the goings over a whisky now and then."

Jordan eyed Farrell somewhat suspiciously as he took his seat. "And what is it you do, Mr. Farrell?" he asked.

"Oh—a little bit of this, a little bit of that, Mr. Jordan," said Farrell, vaguely, pulling his pipe from his pocket and filling it with tobacco from another pocket. "Some would call me a Jack of all trades—or Mick of all trades, more precisely." He grinned. "And what is your occupation, Mr. Jordan?"

Now it was Jordan's turn to be vague. "I've had several occupations in my time."

"Such as?"

Jordan wondered what Farrell's reaction would be if he blurted out the word that had haunted him for months: rebel. Instead, he listed off mechanically, "Printer's devil, fisherman, street sweeper…" he paused for a moment. "Sailor."

Farrell nodded. "A varied career. I see we have that in common, Mr. Jordan."

Jordan did not like the tone of familiarity in Farrell's voice, but said nothing.

Farrell called over to the barkeep. "Gerry—will you bring us two whiskies?" He glanced at Margaret, surmising she could use a drink also. "Make that three whiskies. And tell Billy we'll be having one of his excellent meat pies."

"Yes, sir, Mr. Farrell," said the barkeep, pulling a bottle down from the shelf and pouring their drinks.

Farrell lit his pipe, spitting threads of wayward tobacco out from the corner of his mouth between puffs.

"Now, my dears," he said. "Tell me about your journey."

Margaret looked at her husband, whose menacing expression told her she should keep quiet.

"There's not much to tell, sir," said Jordan, keeping his eyes upon the floor. "We shipped from Cork more than a fortnight ago and arrived here this afternoon."

"Am I to suppose that you plan to make your home in fair New Amsterdam—that you have bid adieu to Ireland forever?" said Farrell, glancing at the bundle of clothes at his feet.

"There was no work for me there. I could not support my family." Jordan had no intention of telling Farrell the true reason for their hasty departure.

Farrell nodded sympathetically. "Again, I see that we have much in common, Mr. Jordan. I left Galway for precisely the same reason—and so have many thousands of our countrymen. It is no wonder that you desired a better life for yourself and your dear ones. Ah! Here we are." He smiled as the three glasses of whisky were brought to their table. "Let us drink to your good health and to that dear island we shall see no more."

He raised his glass and drained it in two gulps. Jordan followed suit, wincing slightly at the unfamiliar burn of the liquor coursing down his throat. Margaret took a sip and began to cough. Farrell laughed.

"I can see you and the whisky are not yet friends, my dear. 'Tis no matter—in truth, were I not so fond of it, I would say that liquor is the devil's urine."

Margaret coughed harder, waking the baby, who began to cry. Gasping for air, she spoke to her husband between coughing spasms.

"I'll go outside 'til I catches my breath and Neddy stops crying. You finish my whisky, but don't eat up my piece of pie when it comes."

"Go on, then, go on," he said dismissively, waving her off.

With Margaret gone from the room, Farrell quickly lost his courtly demeanor.

"Now, Jordan," he said, leaning toward his guest. "There's some things I don't like to speak of with a lady present, but now that you're on my territory, there are a few matters that I wish to discuss with you." He paused, waving at the barkeep for another round of whisky.

"I am the friend and protector of every man who steps off the boat, running from that stinking bitch Ireland and looking for a new life in America," he began. "Don't be fooled, Jordan—New York is a vicious place, and everyone here hates us, from the damnable snobbish knickerbockers who pretends not to remember that their granddaddies were immigrants, to the darkies who wants our jobs at the dockyards. Any one of those bastards would gladly stick a knife in your ribs, just because you was born in Ireland."

Jordan could not conceal his shock.

"Isn't this the country where any man can hope to rise and better himself? Didn't they fight a war to establish real democracy here?"

His words sounded naive even to himself.

Farrell laughed uproariously.

"My God, lad—who told you that? You'd think you'd spent time among those deluded sots who tried to whip the Brits in '98. They were full of big ideas about democracies and all men being equal—what hogwash! Around here, it's every man for himself, and only the strongest survive. And don't let anyone tell you that a kraut, a Jew or a nigger is equal to an Irishman for it's a damned lie!"

Jordan's face flushed at the mention of the rebellion—this was not lost on Farrell.

"Ah! Now I understand, Jordan. Don't think I hold it against you, being a rebel. I hate the English as much as any Irishman. But I was never suicidal enough to join the brotherhood. Why would I risk my life for a country that tried to starve me and my family to death?"

"I never said I was a rebel," protested Jordan feebly.

"You must have made some enemies back home," said Farrell. "Lots did. Many of 'em only joined because they liked the fighting. Many of the ones the Brits didn't hang or cut out their guts in some rat-infested prison yard in Dublin, or Wexford, or Carlow made it over here somehow. Couldn't stand the sight of Ireland, but they still had the fighting spirit. They came in very useful to me."

Farrell smiled broadly, revealing two shining rows of metal teeth.

"You waited longer to leave than most, but I can see you were one of them."

Jordan sat motionless, feeling like a trapped animal. Farrell moved in for the kill.

"How'd you like to work for me? I can find you work immediately and see that your wife and child have a roof over their heads. You'll not get a better offer than that. No reputable man of business in the city will give work to the Irish, particularly those who are fresh off the boat. They consider us carriers of disease, like rats. Until we've been here long enough to establish businesses of our own and undersell the bastards, we must look after our own."

"What kind of work did you have in mind for me?"

"Oh, don't worry—we'll find you something. A man of your skills and experience will fit in anywhere." Jordan was stung by the blatant insincerity in Farrell's voice. "Now Jordan—before your wife comes back and we turn to more pleasant topics, I want your answer. Yes or no?" He held out his hand to Jordan expectantly. Jordan hesitated for several moments before reluctantly shaking the proffered hand.

"Good!" cried Farrell cheerily, spotting Margaret standing awkwardly in the doorway as though waiting to be invited in. He waved energetically at her, calling out in a loud voice, "Come in, my dear, come in! Your husband has just made a wise decision—he has agreed to accept my offer of work and a place to live. Let's celebrate this auspicious meeting—I'll have them mix your next whisky with water and lime to make it go down more agreeably."

Margaret's expression passed from shock to great relief. She ran over to the table and impulsively threw her arms around Farrell's neck.

"I don't know how to thank you, sir. I didn't know what we'd do, being strangers in a strange land. God must have put you in our way just when we were most in need of help."

Jordan pulled her away roughly, his anger piqued by this display. "Sit down, woman, and keep quiet!"

Margaret looked hurt, but her happiness was unchecked.

The meal soon arrived and the Jordans set to with an appetite. They had had nothing to eat but meagre portions of ship's biscuit and water for the past two weeks, and had not tasted meat for many months before that. Farrell watched them eat with a satisfied look on his face. He reflected on how easy it was to ensure a man's services when his belly was empty.

After dinner, he led them to a tall stone building several streets north of the dockyard. It looked far newer and cleaner than any building Ned Jordan had ever lived in. He looked at Farrell with incredulity.

"You own this building?"

Farrell nodded proudly. "I bought the lot from a Dutchman who wished to build a new house on Broadway, and I found plenty of cheap Irish labour to build it."

Jordan was impressed.

"You seem to have done well for yourself."

"Aye, that I have. Now, let me show you your quarters. I have just the spot for you."

The two rooms that Farrell showed them were small, but cozily furnished. Their new floors still smelled of freshly planed pine. Margaret was thrilled.

"Oh Ned, isn't it wonderful?"

Jordan nodded casually, unwilling to appear too enthusiastic.

Farrell smiled, then pulled a pocket watch from his vest, saying, "I must be away. Tomorrow morning I shall arrive at eight sharp to collect Mr. Jordan and introduce him to his new situation. Be sure not to keep me waiting."

"But surely you must live in this fine house yourself?" cried Margaret as he was about to leave.

"No, my dear. I have a house all to myself to live in. This one I keep for the use of my poor countrymen when they are in need of my assistance. Several families are living in the house now; I have found employment for the head of each household. I take great pleasure in being a good Samaritan, you see."

"What a kind man he is! He certainly deserves the gratitude of every Irishman he's helped on his way," said Margaret to her husband after Farrell had left them.

"A man doesn't give more than he expects to receive back," said Jordan with resignation. "He'll find a way for us to pay him back, I am quite sure."

THE NEXT MORNING, Farrell arrived at the boarding house at the appointed hour in a carriage drawn by a fine bay horse. He waved at Margaret, who stood at a second-floor window admiring the carriage that her husband was about to ride in. After his passenger had climbed aboard, Farrell made a clicking noise, and the horse moved on.

"Where are we going?" asked Jordan.

"All in good time, lad—all in good time," replied Farrell.

They drove along the waterfront in an easterly direction where the sun was beginning its steady morning climb. Jordan counted one hundred ships docked on the Manhattan side of the river, and maybe two dozen more on the opposite shore, where churches, houses, and shops attested to the presence of another, smaller city.

"What is its name?" asked Jordan, gesturing to his right.

"The East River."

"No—the name of the city yonder."

"That is Brooklyn, and someday she will surpass even the great city of New York in population and industry."

"What tells you that?"

"Manhattan is an island, and her growth will always be checked by the limits of her geography. Brooklyn does not have such limitations."

Farrell presently turned the horse in a northerly direction. They began to pass more slums, where dirty children huddled in doorways and boards covered windows. Gangs of boys who reminded Jordan of his own childhood in Carlow ran around the carriage, begging for money. Farrell raised his whip at them and shouted, "Out of the way or I'll flay your hides!" The boys rapidly dispersed, uttering curses under their breath.

"Welcome to the Bowery," he said to Jordan. "Your workplace. Today I will have you run some errands for me. Tomorrow I may have something different."

They alit from the carriage, Farrell leading the way into a dingy shop with a torn awning.

"Where's Flaherty?" he demanded abruptly to the sullen-looking stockboy sitting behind the counter, whittling on a stick.

"Down cellar," said the boy. "He's expecting you."

Jordan and Farrell exited the store, and Jordan saw the narrow opening to the cellar covered by two rotten boards. "Go on—open it," said Farrell with impatience.

Throwing aside the boards, Jordan peered down into the abyss-like space below. It was almost completely dark and smelled of mildew. A flimsy ladder extended down into the pit.

"Well, what are you waiting for? Climb down!" ordered Farrell. Jordan reluctantly obeyed. Farrell followed him.

At the back of the cellar, Jordan could see the dim light of a tallow candle burning and could make out three figures sitting at a small table. One stood up and approached them, staggering from the effects of drink.

"Well, well…look what the cat dragged in, boys!"

Jordan felt his face grow hot.

"What we want to know is can he be trusted, Farrell?"

"Oh, I think you'll find he's the trustiest man in the world. He is in my debt and will do as I say, won't you, Jordan?"

"I suppose I have no choice," said Jordan.

Farrell laughed. "There's gratitude for you! Save him from the poorhouse and still he begrudges. We'll have to teach him a few lessons in humility, won't we, boys?"

"Aye, sir," said the two seated figures in unison, jumping almost simultaneously to their feet and seizing upon Jordan, pinning his arms behind his back while the third man drove his first into Jordan's stomach. With a groan, he crumpled onto the floor, while Farrell chuckled above him.

"Ah, 'tis not as bad as all that, laddie. Stand up and shake hands now, like a good sport, and we shall have no more of your impertinence."

When he didn't move, two of the men hauled Jordan roughly to his feet. He could barely breathe, afraid to disturb his throbbing midsection.

"Now, for your first assignment," said Farrell, gesturing to the table where a package lay wrapped in several layers of burlap. "I'll send Flaherty with you to make sure you find the address."

He handed Jordan the burlap bundle. "Take this package to 15 Grand Street—ask for Mac McGoughan. I'll expect you back within two hours. Now get out!"

Jordan painfully climbed up the ladder, blinking in the sunlight. Flaherty tossed the package up to him before climbing up himself and Jordan felt the narrow barrels of several guns wrapped inside. He shivered. What rotten business was this?

Walking along the Bowery on the way to Grand Street, Jordan was shocked by scenes of human misery he thought did not exist in the new world. Dublin and Cork had their slums, to be sure, and Jordan had seen his share of poverty in both places, but part of him could not believe that America shared in this poverty. Wasn't this the country where the streets were paved with gold, the land of opportunity? What could have gone wrong?

At 15 Grand Street, a dilapidated wooden structure passing for a house, the recipient of the package said nothing as Jordan handed him the weapon; he simply handed back a small change purse full of coins and hastily shut the door.

"Give me that," said Flaherty, snatching the purse and pocketing its contents as they walked back to the Bowery. "Farrell's promised me my wages for weeks and never paid yet, damn him."

"What about my share?" asked Jordan plaintively.

Flaherty laughed bitterly. "You'll have to fight for it like the rest of us. Farrell likes to keep us hungry—says it makes us work harder. He's a real son of a bitch, that one."

"Why do you keep working for him, then?" asked Jordan. "Surely there are other jobs in the city."

Flaherty laughed again. "You're new here, so you don't know how things work. No one wants to be on Farrell's black list. He knows everything that goes on in this city—oh yes. He has spies everywhere. He'd think nothing of cutting the throat of a turncoat and tossing him in the river—he's done it several times already."

"How has he avoided getting caught?"

"Do you think the police give a sweet god damn about what the Irish do to each other on the east side? The more that gets killed, the better they like it. We're just like rats to them: something they have to tolerate but are generally disgusted by. You should be sorry you ever came to this rotten city."

Jordan stopped walking. He felt suddenly and utterly exhausted by life and its various forms of cruelty. He longed to be free of it all—the violence, the crowded cities, the poverty and corruption. He closed his eyes, feeling a wave of nausea pass over him. Blocking out the garbage-strewn street on which he stood, he saw clearly in his mind cool blue ocean waters, crisp and inviting. A sailing ship cresting the waves, its white sails billowing like clean sheets on a clothesline. He could see himself on that ship, leaving the squalor behind, bearing north where the human population thinned and was replaced by green forest. It all happened very quickly. Almost before he realized what he was doing, he had grabbed Flaherty by the collar and knocked him to the ground, unconscious. Jordan rummaged through his pockets, retrieved the change purse, and ran toward the waterfront, to the dockyard. He was swallowed up by the fast-moving crowd and was carried along in the current for a time. Had someone seen the robbery? How long would it be before Farrell sent his henchmen after him? His mind racing, Jordan scanned the buildings near the dockyard for Farrell's, where his family would be going about daily tasks. There it was! He sprinted up the narrow street to the front door, bursting in past some women carrying laundry. He found Margaret sitting by the window, mending a tear in a pair of trousers. He struggled to catch his breath.

"Margaret..." he panted. "Farrell...he is not what he seems... he...we must go...leave now."

Margaret looked at Jordan as though he had gone mad.

"Leave? What are you talking about, Ned?" she asked. "He has helped us find a place to live and out of the goodness of his heart has found you a job. Don't tell me that you have had words with him, that he has had to let you go?" Tears welled up in the corners of her eyes. "It is hard, Ned—hard to be your wife. You are always in trouble!"

Enraged by the unfairness of her words, Jordan's hand flew out and struck her across the cheek, leaving a mark.

"Get the baby—we are leaving."

"Have you lost your mind? Where will we go?" She rubbed her cheek, anger spitting from her dark eyes.

"North—to Canada. We cannot stay in this city a moment longer."

Margaret sat down firmly on a chair. "I will not leave! I would rather starve in the street than get on another ship."

Jordan pulled her to her feet by the hair.

"I said we are leaving!" he screamed.

"I will not leave!" Margaret repeated, her voice unwavering.

Jordan's next blow knocked her to the floor, insensible; picking her up, he threw her over his shoulder like a sack of potatoes and grabbed the baby from the wooden crate one of Margaret's neighbours had given her to serve as a crib. With difficulty he struggled out of the building and onto the street once more, where he attracted no more than a passing glance from the bustling crowd. He lurched down to the docks, feeling Margaret stirring on his shoulder after a few minutes.

"Put me down, for the love of God…" she said, faintly. He set her none too gently on her feet, thrusting the baby at her to carry. Margaret looked dazed, as though she were in a nightmare, but dared not stand her ground a second time.

Jordan made for the first ship to catch his eye, a big brigantine. A group of stevedores was engaged in hauling a large number of packing crates aboard her using block and tackle. He approached them.

"When does she sail?"

"Tomorrow morning," replied one of the men, wiping sweat from his forehead.

"Where is she bound?"

"Lower Canada—Quebec City."

Jordan could not believe his luck. He gazed at the ship as a drowning man would at a life raft. He felt the change purse bulging in his pocket and quickly counted out twenty-five, thirty dollars. Would it be enough?

"Is she taking passengers?" he asked the stevedore, who was rapidly losing patience with his interrogation.

"Ask that man—he's the purser, not us."

Jordan looked up and saw the man standing on deck, supervising the loading of provisions. Twenty minutes later, the arrangements had been made. They would sail the next day for Canada.

Chapter 5

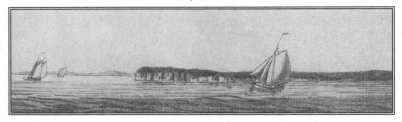

August 26, 1803—

Gravesend
To Mr. Walter Barrell, Director
East India Company
Leadenhall Street, London

Sir—
My name is John Stairs, and I am a nephew of yours, my mother
Joanna and Mrs. Barrell having been sisters while my mother lived.
You may know that their brother John, my uncle, has been so kind
as to foster myself and my sisters and brother in his home in Hali-
fax since the time of our parents' untimely deaths.

I would be in Halifax yet were it not for a most unfortunate
circumstance. My apprenticeship at Mr. Kidston's shop was almost
at an end three months ago, when agents for His Majesty's Navy
seized upon me and one of the junior clerks as we were leaving the
shop for the day. The men would have none of our pleas that we
were bound to Mr. Kidston for a fortnight longer, but brought us
immediately onto His Majesty's Ship *Hussar*—she sailed with the
next day's tide. I will not trouble you with the sad record of my

time as a rating aboard *Hussar*, but would humbly ask your kind assistance in the matter of my obtaining immediate discharge from the Royal Navy. Though I and every good British citizen wish for Bonaparte's immediate demise, I am no fighter.

May I be so bold as to remark that your eminent position with the East India Company would make you an ideal advocate in the matter of my discharge? Any assistance with which you could provide me would be gratefully accepted by your most indebted and obedient nephew,
John Stairs

August 31, 1803
London—

My dear John—
Just in receipt of your letter—an outrageous business, this. You must come to London at once—please find your fare enclosed. The omnibus leaves at six. Come to my office directly. Mrs. Barrell beside herself with excitement at the prospect of seeing Joanna's boy.
Your aff'ct uncle,
Walter Barrell

JOHN STAIRS CLIMBED out of the dark confines of the stage that had carried him to the bustling city of London, his eyes blinking in the sudden light. Before him stood the massive headquarters of the East India Company, its soaring stone pillars and magnificent carvings more reminiscent of a temple or cathedral than of a place of business. The young Stairs had certainly never seen anything like it. As he began his climb up the numerous steps leading to the entrance, he felt like a small insect entering a vast hive of activity. He could not believe that his own uncle was a director in such an enormous enterprise, the company known around the world for its monopoly on trade with India—the reason Britons enjoyed tea and wore silk. It was the East India Company's teas that had been angrily thrown by the crateful into Boston Harbour some thirty years before, and it was the Company's wares that Stairs hoped one day to transport to Halifax when he became a merchant captain. For now, though, there was only one urgent matter preoccupying him: he needed a discharge from the British Navy.

WHEN HE WAS SHOWN into Walter Barrell's cavernous office, Stairs was at first too nervous to speak. His uncle sat behind a large mahogany desk, his face half-hidden behind an enormous globe, its British territories coloured red. Barrell's middle-aged face was round and splotched with red patches something like the globe, attesting to his love of gin. He jumped up from his desk when his nephew was shown in, and hastened to shake the young man's hand.

"Well, well! Joanna's boy—my goodness, but time does fly! How old might you be, lad?"

"Eighteen, sir," replied Stairs, greatly put at ease by his uncle's lack of formality.

Barrell shook his head with apparent disbelief. "I can scarcely believe it. Seems like only yesterday we had the sad news of Joanna's passing, God bless her. But that must be ten years ago now."

Stairs smiled sadly and nodded.

Barrell pulled a well-stuffed chair close to his desk and beckoned for his nephew to sit down. He took his own seat behind the massive desk.

"Now, my lad, shall we get down to business? I was heartily glad to receive your letter, though its contents grieved me much. What sort of lunacy is the navy up to in the colonies, pulling working men from their employments and throwing them aboard those stinking hulks they call warships for no good reason? The whole business is scandalous, I tell you, scandalous!"

Barrell's red face grew redder still as he warmed to his subject.

"If those navy bastards continue on their present course unchecked, there'll be no men left to carry on commerce. Businesses will fail; families will be torn asunder. It's enough to drive a man to drink!"

So saying, Barrell opened a drawer in his voluminous desk and retrieved a large bottle of gin from its depths along with two glasses. He poured out a generous amount and handed it to Stairs, then filled his own glass.

The young man was taken aback; it was only half past nine in the morning. But he drained his glass obediently when his uncle drank to his health and did the same.

"Now, my buck. You can see that there is no love lost between myself and His Majesty's navy. But, of course, I have friends who are not necessarily of the same mind and who will prove helpful in this case."

"I would be eternally in your debt, and theirs, were you able to procure my discharge, Uncle," Stairs said fervently.

"It will be my pleasure to offer what help I can to a promising lad such as yourself," said Barrell, as he picked up his nephew's letter from a pile of papers on his desk and scanned its contents.

"You wrote me, John, that you aspire to become a merchant captain. It seems that life at sea doesn't completely displease you, in spite of your unhappiness in the navy."

"No sir," said Stairs earnestly, beginning now to feel the dizzying effects of the gin. "In fact, in retrospect, I would say the navy has taught me some valuable lessons."

"Oh ? Such as…?" Barrell asked, suspiciously.

"Well—lessons in seamanship, self-discipline, the value of a well-trained crew in dangerous situations."

Barrell nodded, somewhat impatiently. "I must say that it's a credit to you that you are able to see the value in your ordeal, though I must also remark that we would not be engaged in this conversation had you not been so eager to escape from the clutches of the navy. You would likely have been discharged in another year or so in the natural course of things and able to pursue any calling you wished. Was it solely your unhappiness as a rating that brought you here, or have you other reasons for seeking an early release?" Barrell paused, a mischievous look crossing his face. "A young lady back home you hope to marry, perhaps?"

Stairs shifted uncomfortably in his chair.

"Would I were so lucky, sir," he replied hesitantly. "But I do wish to be allowed to return to Nova Scotia and become a merchant captain. The town is growing and there is a great need for goods from New England and overseas. My younger brother has been apprenticed to a merchant in Halifax and someday he hopes to have his own dry goods business, which I could help supply. I lack only the experience, not the will to succeed."

"Ah! Now you're talking sense, boy!" roared Barrell, jumping out of his chair once more and slapping his nephew on the back. "Commerce! That is the foundation of civilization, not these infernal wars! Your brother sounds like a most promising lad; I like your scheme enormously."

Tousling his nephew's hair, Barrell spoke confidingly. "Leave everything to me, John. I'll see to your discharge this very day, and find you a position on one of the Company's ships to get you started."

Stairs grasped his uncle's hand with gratitude.

"My dear uncle, nothing would please me more. I cannot thank you enough for what you have done for me. I shall never forget it!"

"It'll give me pleasure to discomfit the admiral by bringing one of his sailors over to the merchant navy!" Barrell laughed heartily and reached again for the gin bottle.

"Now—let's have another drink, shall we, lad?"

Stairs gulped and nodded bravely.

LATER THAT AFTERNOON, Walter Barrell brought John Stairs to his house in St. James' Square, and for the second time that day, the young man was left speechless by the opulence of the building he was shown into.

His ample Aunt Susannah made a rush for him almost before he had crossed the threshold and lavished him with kisses and embraces that caused him to blush; he was not used to such displays of feminine solicitude.

"Well, Walter—if he isn't the spitting image of his poor mother!" exclaimed Mrs. Barrell with a shrillness that bordered on a shriek. "No doubt about it, my dear boy—you're more Stayner than Stairs!"

Stairs smiled at his aunt, still taken aback by the warmth of his reception.

Looping her arm through his, Mrs. Barrell propelled her nephew inexorably toward the drawing room, and as they entered, Stairs felt himself swallowed up by heavy velvet drapes, brocade-covered furniture and more wealth generally than he had ever dreamed could possibly fit into one room. His aunt continued her oblivious chatter, her plump hand squeezing into his elbow disconcertingly.

"I've had Melinda make tea—you poor thing, I see that the navy has quite starved you. You are altogether too slight for your own good, but a fortnight with Aunt Susannah will cure all that."

The young man Gasped when he saw the number of plates covered with sweets that dotted the tables in the room.

"Really, Aunt Susannah," he stammered, "you have gone to too much trouble on my behalf. I am very sorry for it."

"Nonsense, my dear boy!" shrieked Mrs. Barrell. "Mr. Barrell always takes tea when his business is finished for the afternoon. And even if he did not, how often is it that we have a relative from the other side of the world visit us? Sit down, John dear, and I will pour the tea."

Still feeling the effects of his uncle's gin, the young man dutifully accepted a cup of tea and a butter tart whose sickening sweetness made his stomach lurch. He immediately regretted having eaten it.

"My, my—Walter! What can the navy be thinking, snatching up promising young men like our nephew over in the colonies and forcing them onto those dreadful men-o-war? I grow ill thinking of it! The rats, the filth—not to mention that despicable salt horse they feed the poor boys daily. Small wonder they come home with dysentery and worse! John, dear, you didn't pick up lice while on board ship, did you?"

"Excuse me, Aunt Susannah," Stairs gulped as he rushed for

the front door and vomited into the bushes. Never had the effects of seasickness affected him quite as violently as his aunt's pastries, combined with her views on naval hygiene.

When he returned, quite chagrined, his aunt fluttered over him like a disturbed hen, clucking at him to take some more tea, that was the best thing for upset stomach—and my, wasn't he just like his mother with her delicate stomach?

His head still spinning, Stairs begged leave to lie down, profusely embarrassed by his shameful performance for his wealthy relatives.

"Of course, lad, of course!" bellowed his uncle. "Melinda will make up a bed for you—we expect you will stay with us while I see to your discharge and find you a place on one of our ships."

Stairs spoke weakly, but with profound gratitude. "Nothing would make me happier, uncle."

As he lay in the soft feather bed—indeed, the softest he had ever had the luck to find himself in—Stairs felt a great sense of relief and for the first time in months, fell asleep with a relaxed mind and an optimistic heart.

Chapter 6

May 1808, Quebec City—

Ned Jordan stood on the crest of the high banks of the mighty Saint Lawrence River, near the place where James Wolfe and his invading English army had clambered up the steep cliffs and laid siege to the city nearly fifty years before. It was a wonderful vantage point from which to view the river and its human burden, the many ships that glided smoothly along the river's strong current, bearing goods and passengers into and away from the old French city.

Jordan often came to this place after long, exhausting days on the water, plying his trade as a fisherman aboard whatever ship would have him, chasing the fish that always seemed in short supply. Why was it that every fishing trip he went on seemed to go wrong? Broken tackle, foul weather, small catches—it always seemed to be the same for Ned Jordan. And yet, he was not willing to give up hope of making a living from the ocean, still too much in love with the sense of boundless freedom and adventure promised by that way of life. He could not bring himself to move his family to a big city where he might find work in a mill or a shop; even the prospect brought a sense of despair.

As he watched the passage of seaborne humanity spread out before him, Jordan felt only sadness and the sting of disappointed hope. For the hundredth time, he racked his brain, trying to think of a way—any way—to convince Margaret to leave this place. He had from time to time heard that there was work to be had in Halifax, that its relative proximity to the American colonies would soon make the sleepy little garrison town the queen of the east coast shipping trade, and the idea had soon taken root in his mind. Many times he tried to convince Margaret that moving to Halifax would be the family's financial salvation, but his words always fell on deaf ears. She stubbornly refused to hear of any plan that might bring further instability into her children's lives, believing that the certainty of present misfortune was better than the potentiality of future disaster.

Turning his back on the Saint Lawrence and walking toward the old boarding house whose dinginess and leaking roof contrasted so strongly with the clean and well-lit rooms they might have lived in in New York, Jordan decided that it was worth broaching the subject of moving to Halifax one more time. As soon as he entered the kitchen, he knew that his wife was ill-disposed to listen favorably—or at all—to his old proposal.

A line of washing hung limply over the small stove where Margaret was cooking an even smaller pot of stew from the few scraps she had gotten at the butcher's that morning. Sarah, the couple's third child, fussed continually from her crib near the stove; she was teething and Margaret had not been able to stop her crying for the past two days.

Brushing a lock of hair away from her damp forehead, Margaret tiredly stirred the contents of the stew pot while she spoke to her husband.

"I'll be needing your wages—the children are not getting enough to eat, even though I give them a share of my own plate every night."

"I don't have any money to give you, Margaret—you know that. The fish were not biting this trip and I owe Fraser and Harrison already for the gear I lost two months ago during the storm."

"What are your children going to eat?" said Margaret, her face growing flushed.

Jordan said nothing—truly, he had no idea how they would live through this month.

Finally, he said, "I don't know, but I hear that things are much better in Halifax—it is closer to the Grand Banks and many a man has made his fortune in Nova Scotia."

Margaret shook her head, stirring more vigorously. She had heard this story many times before.

"You'll never be out of debt as long as you live, Ned. It's always the same with you; you'll not be satisfied until you've moved us all the way to Botany Bay, then to the South Pole! You have never been happy with any place we've lived—New York was a fine place, but you were not satisfied there."

Jordan bristled. "'Twas a wicked city, full of misery. I'd not have my children grow up there."

Margaret's retort was sharp as she slammed the lid on the stew pot with a decisive clang. The baby's fussing increased into full-blown cries.

"I've never had a moment's peace with you since the day we left Ireland." She paused. "I know it was the friends of Joe Collins found you the day before we left Cork," she said, with a look of bitter triumph.

Jordan looked aghast—he prided himself on having told his wife very little about his past, and did not know she was aware of his involvement in the rebellion nor of its aftermath.

"What do you mean? Those were men I owed money to in a card game—that's all," he lied. "They threatened to harm you and the baby."

Margaret looked knowing. "You needn't try to deceive me, Ned. I knew when I married you you were a rebel, that you gave up Collins and O'Driscoll for your pardon. It didn't stop me loving you; everyone was mad in those years. Maybe you were never right after '98; it's the only explanation I have for what you've put us through these past years. Why can't you settle somewhere, anywhere, and try to be content?"

Jordan's anger rose up and clutched him at his throat, choking him. "You keep your mouth shut, woman. I've told you how we can be quit of our debts, and you will have none of it. You will not hear of moving elsewhere, of improving our lot. You want me to fail!"

As though she hadn't heard him, Margaret spat out more angry words over the screams of the baby. "It's no use—you'll end your days in a debtors' prison and leave me and the children to starve in the streets."

Jordan's temper flared. "Will you shut that baby up before I strangle it?"

Margaret began to cry. "What'll we do, Ned? The bank owns us lock, stock, and barrel, and we've another baby coming."

The colour drained rapidly from Jordan's face; he looked genuinely horrified.

"God damn it all! Another baby? You've had enough of them already to fill an orphanage."

Margaret spat in disgust.

"'Twas not by my own inclination that I am with child!"

Jordan's face contorted in an angry grimace.

"How I do wish you were barren."

Margaret shot back, "I'll not listen to this a moment longer."

Picking up her sobbing child from its crib, she left the kitchen and carried it into the cramped bedroom where the other two children were huddled silently on their pallet on the floor, fearful of their father's anger. She lay down with them, the baby clutched to her breast. She tried to hide her tears from the children.

"Go to sleep now, Neddy and Maggie. Da's caught no fish today, but he'll be over it by morning."

"Da never catches any fish," four-year-old Neddy's words were muffled, his face pressed against his younger sister's back in the narrow bed.

"Hush, now," said his mother. "Don't let your poor father hear you—do you want him thinking his own son is ashamed of him?"

"I'm not ashamed of Da," Neddy replied, correcting his mother. "But he is the most unlucky man in the world."

Margaret could not help but agree with her oldest child.

THE NEXT DAY, Jordan approached Margaret as she was preparing a breakfast of stale biscuits for the children. He was blunt.

"Come with me to Halifax, or stay here and fend for yourself— I'll have no more of you."

Margaret blanched. "You'd never leave. You wouldn't dare."

"With a wife as faithless as yourself, no man would blame me for leaving."

"What about the children? Do you not care about them?"

Jordan hesitated. Truthfully, he had never even considered the children—so eager was he to be quit of Quebec and the bleak prospects it afforded. He thought about Maggie, his second child and oldest daughter—how her sweet nature and obvious love for her father always charmed and soothed him even when life seemed to be at its worst. Could he live without her? He relented.

"Margaret—it is not my wish to leave for Halifax without you— without the children. But leave I must. There is nothing for it. I believe there is no hope for our family in Quebec. We must go—as soon as we may."

Something in her husband's voice, his attempt at patient explanation of a dire situation, broke Margaret's fighting spirit. She was ready to acquiesce.

"I suppose it is as you say—there is nothing for it. We have been nearly five years here and are no better off than when we first arrived. Surely it can be no worse in Halifax."

"It will be better, Margaret—I promise you. A hundred times better."

With an uncharacteristic rush of emotion, Ned Jordan caught his wife in his arms and held her tightly while her arms wrapped around his neck in a stranglehold. They clung together in this way for several minutes.

Chapter 7

June 1808, Halifax, Nova Scotia—

Jordan walked briskly along the cobbled streets of Halifax, where the bustle of the business day had already begun. Passing by the base of George Street, Jordan glanced at the elegant clock that stood watch over the town from the slopes of Citadel Hill; nine o'clock already! Where had the morning gone? He had left Margaret and the children asleep at the boarding house as the dawn was breaking, and slipped out the door before Mrs. Zinck, the proprietress, could corner him and demand payment for their room and board these past two weeks. He had been putting her off for days now, assuring her that the rent would be forthcoming as soon as other debts were paid, assurances that Mrs. Zinck regarded with well-founded suspicion. Accustomed for years to living on the verge of starvation, Jordan had altogether lost any sense of shame about making promises he could not keep—ethical considerations were a luxury afforded only to the wealthy, in his view. Over the last ten desperate years of his life, Jordan had hardened into the kind of cold and driven man who would say and do anything for money. That extreme poverty, and not avarice, had occasioned this transformation in his character did not mitigate this change in Jordan. He had few joys in his life now, and because sleep often eluded him, spent several hours of each morning walking through the Halifax streets, lost in thought, as he was doing today. Worries preoccupied him. How he feared for his children—his daughters especially—when he thought of what the future might hold in store! Daughters of a once-condemned and perpetually indebted Irish refugee, their prospects seemed bleak indeed. But then, all might yet be well, for Maggie, the eldest, was beautiful. Her black hair and startling doe-like features would make for her a good marriage, one that might raise the family's fortunes. Jordan clung to this hope as a drowning man clutches at a lifeline.

MAGGIE! Born shortly after he and Margaret had come to Quebec from New York, the little girl had always been the apple of her father's eye. Though he largely ignored her older brother, Neddy, whom he viewed as just a sad copy of himself, Jordan doted on Maggie when he came home after his fishing trips, and would play with her by the hour, revealing a patience and kindness that his wife had almost forgotten he ever possessed. She was a happy child, content to play with a wooden spoon or a piece of yarn, for there were never any toys. Margaret taught her songs from the old country, and even when she was very young, Maggie loved to sing for her father.

"Listen, Da," she would say, crawling into his lap and beginning to sing, "I had a ship in the northern country, She goes by the name of the Golden Vanity. I'm afraid she'll be taken by some bold Roosian crew as she lies on the lowlands, on the lowlands, as she lies on the lowlands low."

Jordan caught her up in an embrace just tight enough to make her squeak with discomfort, then kissed her soft cheek, saying, "You are a wonder, child. You will make your husband very happy someday."

Maggie looked indignant. "No husband, Da!"

Her father laughed uproariously. "No husband? What ails you, child? Do you want to stay at home with your Ma and Da forever?"

Maggie nodded vigorously, grinning.

Jordan kissed her again. "Sweet child, 'twould be a great comfort to have you look after me in my old age. But some man will take you from me; your beauty will not let us keep you long."

Maggie giggled. "Not beautiful, Da—plain as water. Neddy told me."

Jordan scowled in his son's direction. "Boy—don't let me ever catch you saying such things to your sister." Neddy looked fearful.

Turning his attention back to his favourite child, Jordan stroked her hair, musing, "Will it be a duke for Maggie Jordan's husband, or the captain of a fine sailing ship? A lord of the manor? A prince?"

Maggie piped up, "A fisherman!"

Jordan scowled again. "No, no! Not a fisherman—he'll keep you in rags, eating fish head soup with twenty brats to care for."

In fact, Maggie very much enjoyed fish head soup and did not mind wearing rags.

She nodded decisively. "A fisherman for Maggie's husband—just like Da."

Jordan's eyes filled with tears as Maggie comforted him.

WITH THOUGHTS OF MAGGIE still playing in his mind, Jordan turned the corner onto Water Street, where wooden warehouses and sturdy granite ship chandleries clustered along the waterfront. It was a world he loved and understood from his days of fishing along the St. Lawrence. Being a fisherman had taught him much about the necessities a man required for a long and dangerous voyage in a small boat, knowledge that he would need for his present endeavor to succeed. He scanned the shopfronts for a signboard reading "Jonathan and John Tremaine, chandlers"—there it was! Stopping a moment to check his appearance reflected in the shop window, he opened the door and entered the shop. A clerk who had been writing in a ledger behind the counter looked up as he approached.

"A good morning, sir," said Ned Jordan.

"And to you, sir," said the clerk.

"Might I speak with one of the owners of this fine establishment?"

"Indeed you may, sir. One moment please." The clerk disappeared through a doorway behind the counter that was almost completely concealed by a row of hanging oilskins. Jordan breathed in the familiar smells of every ship chandlery he had ever known: a pleasantly astringent mixture of Stockholm tar, chewing tobacco and coal smoke.

In a few minutes, the clerk returned with his employer Jonathan Tremaine, a lean, sober-faced man of New England extraction. Stepping out from behind the counter, Tremaine smiled pleasantly and grasped Jordan's hand with a firmness that almost made him flinch.

"A good morning to thee, sir," he said, bowing slightly.

"And to you, my dear sir," replied Jordan, puzzled slightly by Tremaine's archaic speech. He remembered later that the Tremaines were Quakers.

"And what may we do for thee?" asked the tall New Englander.

"Well, sir, I am in the fishing business, and am aiming to build me a schooner. I've already three hundred quintals of cod drying out in barrels at Gaspé and the prospect of several hundred more this season, if the weather holds. These I can offer you by way of insurance if you will help me build her."

Tremaine nodded sagely, then spoke.

"I see that thou art a man of some means. Shall we retire to my office and discuss thy plans further? James—summon me if Mr. Hogg returns for his sailcloth."

"Yes, sir," said the clerk, standing up and moving his stool so that the two men could pass behind the counter and through the door to the Tremaines' office.

Fifteen minutes later, they had agreed to the terms of Jordan's loan and had shaken hands upon it. Like most merchants in the chandlery business, the Tremaines were used to fishermen borrowing against the next season's catch, and perhaps because they were God-fearing men, their rates of interest always remained low.

It was not Christian to extort money from honest, hard-working men with families to support.

For his part, Jordan left the store with a heart lightened at the prospect of his new venture, and only slightly concerned about the lie he had told Jonathan Tremaine about those three hundred quintals of fish in Gaspé. He felt sure that, once she was built, his schooner would pay for herself. He only needed a bit of help getting started. Gone were the days of fishing on another man's boat, of dreaming of a life spent sailing the ocean! Now he would be able to hire his own crew—maybe even offer some unfortunate Irishman an honest job aboard his ship. He fairly skipped back up the hill to the boarding house, bursting to tell Margaret and the children the good news.

He knew something was amiss as soon as he entered the house. Running up the stairs to their three cramped rooms, he saw Margaret weeping over Maggie's bed and being comforted by the landlady, Mrs. Zinck, the other children hushed and huddled in a far corner of the front room, as far away from their sister as possible. The little girl lay on her stomach, her back and right arm heavily bandaged. Her breathing was laboured.

Jordan stared in disbelief at his stricken daughter.

"What happened?" he called out weakly to the women who hovered over the sickbed.

"I told her and told her and Neddy not to play around the fire," said Margaret in a strangled voice. "But they didn't mind me. She must have caught her foot on the mat and fallen in. I was in the other room feeding little Rosie when I heard her screaming. When I pulled her out of the fireplace, her clothes were all ablaze. I wrapped her up in the mat and rolled her around until the fire was out…"

Mrs. Zinck spoke. "I've sent for the doctor, Mr. Jordan. He should be here presently. I tore up an old sheet to make bandages. She's badly burned her back and arm."

Jordan felt as if he would faint and propped himself against the nearest wall for support. How could everything have gone so wrong, so quickly? Three short hours ago, he had looked in on Maggie, beautiful in her sleep as she always was, and had kissed her and her sisters tenderly before leaving for his appointment with the Tremaines. Was this latest misfortune yet another manifestation of the ill luck that seemed to follow him wherever he went? He closed his eyes and saw Collins' contorted face leering at him from a Wexford gallows, then opened them again to his terribly wounded daughter. Would she live, and if she lived, would she ever be beautiful again? Jordan felt all his dreams for a beloved daughter come crashing down around him. He could not bear to hear the doctor's verdict, but ran from the house, unable to stifle his sobbing.

MAGGIE JORDAN stayed in bed for most of the summer, her small body swathed in bandages. Her mother changed and washed them daily, which added to her daily burden of diapers and other washing she took in for the landlady to help defray the family's living expenses. Maggie's burns slowly lost their frightening purple colour, but it soon became obvious that her arm had suffered badly and that it would remain permanently withered, a fact which did not seem to dampen the little girl's spirits.

"Don't worry, Da," she said to her sorrowing father. "Now there will be no husband and I'll be able to take care of you when you grow old."

Jordan's heart was broken. He could no longer take pleasure in dreams of a wealthy marriage for his favorite child, and spent most of his time away from the house where she was confined.

"Don't let the neighbours see her," he told Margaret. "I'll not have them calling my child a cripple."

Margaret nodded, tears in her eyes.

Jordan grew to hate coming home in the evening, where an atmosphere of gloom prevailed. The other children were sombre and he often caught looks of silent recrimination in Margaret's eyes. Even Rosie, the new baby, seemed afraid to cry too loudly around her father. Jordan felt like a man walking in a nightmare with no sense of direction, not caring what might happen to him.

He talked to the Tremaines about building his ship not at the Halifax yard, as he had planned, but in Gaspé, telling them labour would be cheaper there. The merchants guessed the real reason for the change in plans: they had heard about Jordan's late misfortune, and were sympathetic to his desire to leave Halifax for a time. To Jordan's relief, they were also willing to give him extra time to fulfill his obligations to the firm. Going to Quebec, they reasoned, would give Jordan time to collect the fish he owed them. But the Tremaines were no fools. Guessing at Jordan's true financial situation, they asked for an additional security. Before Jordan left Halifax, they had him mortgage his still-to-be-constructed ship to them, something he did with reluctance. With additional store credit, Jordan bought the necessaries for his trip to Gaspé and some of the materials needed for the construction of the schooner. Then, one crisp September morning when Maggie was well enough to leave her bed, he announced to Margaret that they would be leaving for Gaspé. His wife was caught completely offguard.

"What madness is this, Ned Jordan? We've not been in Halifax five months," she sputtered in disbelief. "Your ship is not even on the stocks and Maggie's still unwell."

"I can have her built more cheaply in Quebec," Jordan lied. "We will be there only for the winter. Then, when she's launched, we'll sail her back to Halifax with enough cod to keep the Quakers happy."

"Winter in Gaspé?" said Margaret with horror. "We'll not survive it, Ned. 'Twas bad enough in Quebec when every night for six months I thought we'd freeze to death. You don't know what it was like—you were off in that boat of yours. But I remember, oh yes, only too well!"

"I told you we'll only be there until the ship is built. Then we'll return to Halifax or anywhere you please."

"What makes you think anyone in Gaspé will extend you credit after the way we left Quebec? Do you think word hasn't travelled?"

Jordan's eyes sparkled with anger. "The bastards in Quebec took my gear! I owe them nothing. They were just a damned bunch of bankers and no-account shopkeepers who never did a tap of work in their lives. It will be different in Gaspé; there are real boatbuilders and fishermen there who understand how hard it is to make a living from the ocean."

"I don't see how it will ever be any different for you, Ned."

Jordan looked at his wife for a long time.

"Margaret," he began. "I know I have asked much of you these past years, that I have brought you much unhappiness. You must believe that I am trying to remedy all that—to be a better breadwinner for you and the children. With my own schooner and a small crew, I will be able to bring in the kind of catches that will provide for us. And I have friends from Gaspé who can help me build *Three Sisters* and get her launched." For the first time, Jordan called his ship by the name he had chosen for her many weeks ago.

"*Three Sisters?*" Margaret looked puzzled, then her face burst into a smile, something her husband had not seen for a very long time. "Oh! Ned—for our girls?"

Jordan nodded.

"Girls, do you hear? Your father has named his ship for you." Margaret's eyes were shining with tears.

"A ship for us! A pretty ship for us!" cried Maggie and Sarah, dancing around their father's legs.

With her good arm, Maggie embraced her father.

"Thank you, Papa," she whispered.

Clasping his daughter fiercely, Jordan burst into tears.

CONSTRUCTION OF *THREE SISTERS* began soon after the family's arrival in Gaspé late in September. To Jordan's relief, the weather stayed good well into November and the keel was laid before the first snow squalls blew in from the north. He stayed at the dockyard from early in the morning until sundown, meekly taking orders from the foreman, endlessly sawing, planing, hammering, caulking. He picked up bits and pieces of French from the building crew and provoked great mirth at the dockyard the first time he was heard to yell "*Tabernacle!*" when the mallet hit his finger instead of the nail.

Jordan took a proprietorial pride in every detail of *Three Sisters*, from the kind of timber and rope used for her masts and rigging to the colour she should eventually be painted. When the foreman informed him in broken English that work on the ship would cease until the spring, Jordan could barely stifle his impatience. He visited her every day that winter, peeking under her canvas tarpaulin with secret satisfaction on his way to the general store where he had found temporary work stocking shelves and counting inventory. He dreamed of her, completed, several times a week—her name proudly displayed on her bow. To Jordan, the ship represented the freedom and independence he had always wished for and never found. She was truly the great love of his life.

When *Three Sisters* finally slid from the stocks and into Gaspé Bay in April of the following year, the entire Jordan family turned out to see her. The Jordan girls were especially excited at the launching of their namesake, clapping their hands with glee and jumping up and down in such a frenzy that their mother was afraid all three would fall into the drink with the ship. Jordan himself stood beaming in silent admiration, though he was deeply troubled by the almost insurmountable hole he had dug himself, as building costs had risen beyond even his most liberal estimates, plunging him still further into debt. He had resisted the urge to ornament *Three Sisters* with a figurehead, though his daughters had begged him for one. A working ship, she had no gallery at her stern, nor any cabin windows except for the skylight that allowed light into the small cabin.

Jordan was extremely proud of his tub-shaped ship—all forty-five-and-a-half feet, sixty-four tonnes of her. What difference did it made if she was rather broad in the beam? She would need to be capacious to hold the fish her owner was sure she would soon be transporting to markets from Montreal to Halifax. When it came time to paint her, Jordan chose black and yellow, the cheapest colours he could find. With wide yellow stripes running along the sides of her wide black body, *Three Sisters* had the look of a large bumblebee. He told himself that beauty was not everything—she was to be a working ship, after all, and so would have to forgo a lady's vanities.

As he stood silently admiring his new ship, Jordan felt a small hand slipped confidingly into his.

"She's beautiful, Da," said Maggie, smiling. "The most beautiful ship that's ever been built."

Chapter 8

April 1809, Halifax, NS—

William Kidston drew a sharp breath as he crossed the threshold of the Masonic Hall; though the prosperous merchant had often attended balls and banquets held at the hall in the past, this evening promised to put all of her former glories to shame.

Just a few days ago, the province's governor, Sir George Prevost, had sailed into Halifax Harbour in triumph after having participated in the British attack on the Caribbean island of Martinique, wresting control of the island and its rich sugarcane plantations away from Napoleon Bonaparte and his French forces—a well-publicized triumph in both London and the colonies. Proud of their gallant governor and his victory over the little French tyrant before whom nations trembled, the merchants of Halifax, among whom William Kidston was a prominent member, had agreed to host a soiree at the well-appointed Masonic Hall to celebrate his achievement. Four hundred distinguished guests had been invited to attend, including the officers of His Majesty's ships *Eolus*, *Cleopatra* and *Centurion*, in whose company Prevost had made the journey to the Caribbean. The cream of Halifax society would be in full display this evening, and Kidston smiled to himself when he thought of the twittering and squawking of the female members of that society in their finest plumage, begowned and bejewelled, ready to commence a cutting, whispered commentary on each other, safely tucked behind colourful paper fans.

"May I take your coat, sir?" asked a footman in a red suit and white gloves as Kidston stood in the foyer, amid a crush of others, waiting to pass into the main part of the hall. The sound of a string quartet could be heard above the din of voices wafting from the hall. As he removed his coat and handed it to the footman, Kidston issued him a stern warning. "Make sure not to lose it, mind!"

Though one of the wealthiest of Halifax's merchants, the fifty-year-old Scot had never lost his keen appreciation for the value of a dollar. Some might even have called him parsimonious, an appellation Kidston largely ignored.

Passing beneath a wide arch made from entwined evergreen boughs dotted with tiny pink mayflowers, Kidston breathed in the pleasantly astringent aroma of spruce mixed with the fresh scent of the mayflowers, just at their best at that time of year. Pausing just beyond the arch, he looked around the crowded hall in amazement. Painted figures of the King's arms and various allegorical representations of British military glory covered the walls of the spacious room: here, a soldier and a sailor shook hands while a beaming Lady Britannia looked smilingly on; there, Britannia proudly waved her ensign over the head of Time, holding History in his hand while revealing to Posterity the amazing record of the conquest of Martinique. Nearby, life-sized paper cutouts of Prevost and his officers painted in full military regalia supervised the ostentatious scene with apparent satisfaction. The spoils of war, an assortment of swords and bloodied flags seized from the French at the battle of Fort Bourbon, were amassed in a place of prominence where their presence elicited many favourable comments.

As he contemplated this rich display, Kidston heard a whistle and turned to see his friend and fellow merchant Edward Albro approaching through the crowd, a glass of red wine in his hand.

"Quite a show, wouldn't you say, Bill."

"I'll say it is! How much will this cost us, do you imagine?"

"A thousand, at least, but what does that matter? We can certainly afford it, and it cannot but be good for our business to make the acquaintance of a few more navy captains and their retinues. The navy will always need its supplies—and we'll always be here to provide 'em."

"Aye, that we will, Ned, that we will."

Kidston lit his pipe and puffed thoughtfully, nodding at his friend's assessment.

His own business in ships' hardware, liquor, and cotton had grown over the past decade to include a thriving overseas timber trade. He would never feel the pinch of poverty as long as Glasgow needed wood for its buildings and sailors liked their drink. Still, excess galled him—and no one could deny the excessiveness displayed in the Masonic Hall on this occasion.

"I shudder to think of what they've cooked up for our meal."

"More than a meal, my friend—it's a veritable feast, I assure you. Nothing but the best for our gallant governor and his conquering heroes. Speaking of whom, has the guest of honour arrived yet?"

"I have not laid eyes on him, but I only just arrived myself."

Albro nodded, sipping his glass of wine.

"While I have you here, Bill, there's a matter that I've been meaning to bring to your attention for some time—I've been too preoccupied lately with orders for the spring season to pay you a call. Do you object to discussing business for a moment?"

"Not a bit," said Kidston.

"Good. Last summer, I had dealings with an Irishman by the name of Jordan who bought some gear from me on credit that he never paid. Now the Tremaines tell me that he's gone off to Quebec to build himself a schooner—with their money. I say they are fools, but leave that aside for the moment. The debt Jordan owes me is sizeable, and I have no way of ascertaining if he plans to pay it back. John Tremaine tells me they hold the deed to this ship, if it ever gets built. Have you had dealings with this Jordan?"

Kidston's face creased into a scowl at the mention of Jordan's name.

"Aye, I have. He came to my shop last June asking for a loan; I didn't like the cut of his jib. Still, I agreed to lend him a few pounds to buy nets and rope, I believe it was. It does not surprise me to hear that he's left for Quebec. He probably owes money to half the merchants of Halifax."

While Kidston was speaking, Albro caught sight of Jonathan Tremaine a few paces away, his plain, homespun coat sticking out like a sore thumb among the rich fabrics and expensive uniforms that surrounded him. He looked awkward and uncomfortable.

"Look, Bill," said Albro. "There's Tremaine now—just the man we need presently. He must have just arrived. Jonathan!" he called out to Tremaine, waving his hand. "Do come join us!"

The lanky Quaker looked relieved, and crossed the floor to join the two men.

"A good evening to thee," he said, bowing politely.

"And to you, Jonathan," said Kidston, before cutting to the chase. "We were just speaking about what a Christian gentleman you have shown yourself in your dealings with Ned Jordan."

Tremaine again looked uncomfortable.

"It was my brother John who had dealings with Mr. Jordan, and not I."

Kidston nodded. It was a well-known fact among Halifax merchants that John Tremaine was the more generously disposed of the two brothers. He continued.

"Yes. Mr. Albro and I are both owed money by this Irishman, and we would like to know where we might find him in order to collect it. We know you have generously agreed to help him build a schooner, and that he has been living in Quebec of late."

Tremaine looked still more uncomfortable.

"Yes, he is living in Gaspé. He wished to leave Halifax for a time—his little girl was badly burned at the house where he was living, and there are good boatbuilders in Quebec, as you know. We have not heard from Jordan in several months." He paused.

"But we had him mortgage the ship to us and have every intention of seizing her should he not be able to pay back his debt."

The merchants' conversation was interrupted by a loud trumpet fanfare as Sir George Prevost and his wife made a grand entrance into the hall, accompanied by the captains of the three British frigates in full dress uniform, their medals glinting in the lamplight. After the small procession had taken its place at the head of the hall, great quantities of wine were poured and there began a series of toasts to Prevost and his men, to the King and his great navy, and to the merchant hosts.

A few moments later, the crowd parted and a furious murmuring began as a new wonder was brought into the magnificent hall.

"Would you look at that?" said Albro to Kidston as a footman staggering under a huge platter of oddly shaped pastry wove his perilous way through the crowd toward the head table. Another footman followed with a knife.

"What is it?" asked Kidston, craning his neck for a better view.

"I do believe it is a representation of Fort Bourbon, lately captured in Martinique, in pastry," said Tremaine, dubiously. "I heard Mr. Hartshorne and Mr. Boggs talking about it with great excitement. They seem to think it a remarkable likeness."

"Well I'll be damned! A pastry fort—whatever can we expect next?" said Albro, shaking his head.

The giant platter having been set down before Prevost, with great ceremony the governor sliced into the Fort, sending its walls tumbling into a shower of crumbs, which he wiped daintily from his fingers with a linen handkerchief. A loud cheer arose from the crowd, followed by the cry, "Down with Bonaparte! Let tyrants ever be served thus!"

Kidston had a sudden feeling of claustrophobia; the room seemed to have suddenly grown very hot and he felt dizzy. The chattering voices that surrounded him were loud and frenetic. Had they had too much to drink, or had he?

"Gentlemen, if you will excuse me. I am not feeling well, and must take my leave of you."

Albro and Tremaine looked concerned.

"May I accompany thee out of the hall and see that thou find a carriage?" asked the Quaker merchant.

"Thank you kindly, but I think I will take the air and walk home. But before I leave, may I ask that you inform me the moment you receive word that Jordan is returning to Halifax?"

Tremaine nodded. "Indeed I will."

"Make sure I am not the last to hear when he arrives back in Halifax—if he ever does. I have some choice words for the Irishman!" Albro added, darkly.

Kidston bowed to his two colleagues and hastily exited the room. He did not wish to stay to the end, knowing that such events regularly continued on into the early hours of the morning.

Indeed, it was four a.m. when the last guests staggered from the hall, flush with wine and dizzy from dancing. All agreed that the evening had been a stunning success.

June 1809, Schooner Three Sisters—

NED JORDAN STOOD PROUDLY at the wheel of his new ship as her mainsail caught a sudden gust of wind and billowed out like a swan unfolding its powerful wings. He could not believe that *Three Sisters* was really built, that she was no longer just a figment of his imagination but an actual vessel made of wood and canvas. Grasping her wheel, he felt an almost giddy exhilaration—that anything he chose to put his mind to was possible. He could not remember ever feeling happier.

They were making good progress and it would be only a few more days before they reached Halifax, having left Gaspé three days ago. Jordan had employed two of the boys from the dockyard to help him sail *Three Sisters* to Nova Scotia. Though not much older than Neddy, both had worked on ships before, and were capable seamen.

Looking toward the bow, Jordan could see Maggie jumping up and down with excitement, pointing at something in the water.

"It's a whale!" the six-year-old shouted at her brother with glee. "He's heard about our lovely ship and wants to see her for himself."

Neddy sniffed contemptuously at his sister. "No he hasn't—and if I had a harpoon, I'd kill him."

Maggie looked horrified. "Oh, why?"

"For his oil; everyone knows that every lamp in Boston's lit with whale oil."

Maggie looked disgusted, then incredulous. "You have some very strange ideas, Neddy. I don't believe a word of what you say."

Neddy shrugged and was silent; girls were silly, stupid creatures, in his view, and did not understand the ways of the world like men did. He considered himself extremely unlucky to have three sisters and no brothers to play with.

AFTER TWO DAYS of keeping a southwesterly course down the Nova Scotia coastline, Jordan spotted the Sambro light through his spyglass at a distance of several miles, and had *Three Sisters* brought around in a northwesterly direction heading into Halifax Harbour. As they drew close to McNab's Island, Maggie was the first to see the gallows standing guard over a small beach, its prey dangling in the wind. She grasped her mother's hand, and asked, "What did that man do?"

"He must have been wicked," Margaret replied.

"What wicked things did he do?"

"He might have been a thief, or a murderer. There are many kinds of wickedness in the world for which a man may hang."

"Why did they leave him there and not bury him?" asked Neddy, whose sense of the rightful order of things was offended by the sight of the rotting corpse.

"It's meant as a warning," said Jordan, his mind racing back to the heads he had once seen piked on a Carlow bridge after the rebellion. "So that other men will not steal nor murder."

Neddy looked quizzically at his father.

"Have you ever gone to a hanging?"

Jordan thought about his narrow escape from the gallows, something he would never tell his son about.

"No, lad. But I know that not every man who hangs is guilty, and that there are plenty of thieves who die in their beds."

Neddy nodded sagely. He knew from experience that life was full of unfairness.

As they passed into the inner harbour, Jordan pointed *Three Sisters* in the direction of the Tremaines' wharf, where supplies for their nearby shop were regularly unloaded. Once the ship had been made fast to the wharf, he disembarked, eager to pay a call to the Tremaines and show them the ship.

"Well, well—Mr. Jordan," said John Tremaine when Jordan was brought into his office. "We thought for a while we'd seen the last of thee—that thou had made for the high seas."

"Would I serve men who have shown me such kindness in that way?" replied Jordan, stung by a kernel of seriousness in Tremaine's joking remark.

"I have some rather bad news, I'm afraid. My brother has spoken with Mr. Kidston and Mr. Albro. They have inquired about thy whereabouts and how they might reach thee regarding some outstanding debts accrued at their places of business last year."

Jordan felt his face redden. He said nothing.

"My brother told them that thou'd travelled to Gaspé with thy family, and that thou were in the process of building a schooner, for which we held the bill of sale. We reassured them that we looked for thy return as soon as the ship was built, to settle thy accounts. This reassurance, however, did nothing to satisfy the gentlemen."

Tremaine paused, looking Jordan straight in the eye.

"Now that thou art in Halifax, they have promised to have thee arrested and to seize whatever property they find in thy possession, as payment."

Jordan swallowed hard. How short a distance it was from the

wharf to the poorhouse, from prosperity to utter ruin! He could find no words with which to reply.

After an awkward silence, John Tremaine asked, "Does *Three Sisters* carry any cargo presently which may serve to satisfy the gentlemen?"

Jordan shook his head. "None, sir."

Tremaine folded his thin arms across his chest "In that case, I have no choice but to inform Messrs. Albro and Kidston that there is nothing for them—they will, no doubt, proceed with their action against thee."

Seized with a sudden panic, Jordan dropped to his knees at Tremaine's feet, grasping his ankles in a gesture of submission. The merchant looked shocked.

"Please, Mr. Tremaine, sir—I am a man facing ruin, which were not so bad but for my wife and children, who do not deserve the poorhouse. 'Tis I have been cursed with terrible luck all my life, while they have been cursed to depend on such a beggar as I. Can you find it in your heart to pay my debt to Albro and Kidston while I find a crew for the fishing season? I swear to you, on the souls of my daughters, I will not fail you! No, not this time. I am determined to overcome my luck and to satisfy all my creditors as soon as I am able. Mr. Tremaine, please—will you help me?"

John Tremaine had never witnessed such a spectacle, and certainly never in his own place of business.

"Get up off the floor, I beg thee, Mr. Jordan," said Tremaine, rising swiftly to his feet and stepping back from the groveling man before him. "There is no need for such a performance."

Jordan stood up, his head bowed with sincere chagrin.

"Those three hundred quintals of fish we agreed upon some months ago, I presume, are no longer in your keeping?"

Jordan nodded guiltily, remembering his earlier dissimulation.

"Have thou no assets of any kind left in Gaspé—no one who owes thee a favour? Think carefully, Mr. Jordan."

Jordan thought of the hundred quintals of salt cod he knew would be sitting in the warehouse of Daniel Johnson, the Perce merchant he had worked for when he crewed aboard one of Johnson's fishing schooners two years ago. Johnson was prosperous and his storehouses always seemed to be bulging at the seams—and he was one of the few merchants of his acquaintance of whom Jordan had not yet asked a favour. Would Johnson agree to supply him with the fish to buy off his present creditors if Jordan promised him a share of the season's catch aboard *Three Sisters*? Knowing Johnson's parsimonious nature, Jordan seriously doubted it. Still, desperate to offer Tremaine something, anything—Jordan began to spin his lie. "There is a merchant, in Perce, by the name of Johnson with whom I had dealings for several years. When times were hard and money was tight, some of us who crewed on his schooner agreed to forgo our wages with the promise that we would be paid when catches were better. As for me, I could not take bread from a man's mouth—I had other irons in the fire... "

He waved his hand in the air with a flourish of generous forbearance, warming to the virtuous, though entirely fictional portrait he was painting of himself.

"Margaret brought in washing and we managed. When *Three Sisters* was finished, I was anxious to bring her to Halifax to show you and the other Mr. Tremaine, and to start fishing as soon as I could to repay my debt to you. In truth, I had almost forgotten the quintals of fish waiting for me at Johnson's warehouse."

John Tremaine looked incredulous.

"How many, Mr. Jordan?"

"Two hundred, sir. Not enough to repay my full account, but a start, at least. Had I thought of them in time, I would surely have stopped in Perce and loaded them on; my mind was too preoccupied with other matters, such as navigating the ship. With your kind forbearance, sir, I would be happy to sail back to Quebec at the earliest possible date, and fetch that fish back to Halifax for Kidston and Albro."

Tremaine sighed. Jordan was hopeless, that much was certain. But the merchant's fortunes were now tied to the Irishman, and though Tremaine strongly suspected he was being lied to, he maintained a perverse sympathy for Ned Jordan. He seemed not to be able to get out of his own way, yet Tremaine could not find it in himself to send him packing off to debtors' prison. John Tremaine knew he would have a fair amount of explaining to do to his less sympathetic brother when he arrived in the afternoon, but for the moment, he extended his hand to Jordan one more time:

"All right, Mr. Jordan—all right. I will see that thou receive the necessaries for thy trip to Perce. And I will see to the matter of thy account with Mr. Kidston and Mr. Albro."

Jordan shook the proffered hand warmly. "I am eternally grateful to you, Mr. Tremaine. You are fine Christian gentlemen, you and your brother. God bless you."

With that, a relieved Ned Jordan took his leave of the Tremaines.

Chapter 9

July 15, 1809

Halifax—

Dear friend John,
My brother has contracted with Ned Jordan to ship two hundred
quintals of fish from Mr. Johnson's storehouse in Perce to us, to
serve as payment for his sizable debts. Thou may remember, he is
the builder of the schooner *Three Sisters* from Gaspé, now docked
at our wharf.

Will thou do us the great favour of accompanying Mr. Jordan
to Perce and returning with the fish? My brother has placed his
trust in Mr. Jordan, but I have strong reservations as to the man's
character. Should thou not find the amount of fish he claims to
have in Mr. Johnson's storehouse, would thou bring us back the
difference, up to a total of five hundred quintals, for we are short
here?

Come to the office and we will see thee furnished with the necessaries for thy voyage.
Jonathan Tremaine

Tremaine called for his errand boy to deliver the letter to Mr. John Stairs of Hollis Street.

That afternoon, the young captain paid a call to Tremaine and Tremaine. He had already visited the wharf where *Three Sisters* was docked, and had chuckled at her clownish appearance. "A wallowing sow," he thought to himself. "She likely handles like one." He was used to the Gaspé schooners with their high sides and wide bottoms, built for the transportation of the greatest possible amount of cargo and passengers. He would accept the commission as a favour to the Tremaines, who had always treated him well; as a boy, he used to love climbing on the huge piles of sweet-smelling rope in their warehouse and he had once confided to them his dream of becoming a merchant captain. Now twenty-four and finally in possession of his master's ticket, thanks in large part to the good offices of his well-connected uncle, John Stairs was familiar with life at sea and had already had several commissions from other Halifax merchants. His younger brother William had finished his seven-year apprenticeship at Kidston's hardware shop and ship chandlery, and was now eyeing a building on the corner of George Street and Bedford Row that would make an excellent store of his own, well situated near the waterfront where John's vessels could supply him with imported merchandise. But all of that was for the future: for the present, John Stairs was happy to serve as the Tremaines' agent; he was sure he could handle this Ned Jordan fellow and his *Three Sisters*. Running his hand through his sand-brown hair, which rather needed trimming, Stairs entered the Tremaines' store and was shown into the office.

The two sober-faced Quakers were waiting for him.

"Ah, John—welcome!" said Jonathan, rising to shake the young man's hand. "We thank thee for thy promptness."

"Good day to you, sirs," Stairs replied with a courteous bow. "I came as soon as I had your letter."

The merchants eyed their visitor expectantly. Stairs continued.

"I would be honoured to serve as your agent on *Three Sisters*. I have just had a look at her now, and am at your disposal whenever you choose to have her sail."

The brothers looked relieved.

"Thy words are a great comfort to us, John," said Jonathan. "We are in some doubt as to Mr. Jordan's state of affairs at present." Here Jonathan's expression turned to one of long-suffering as he looked over at his brother. "Should any troubles arise, therefore, we would ask thee to execute this bill of sale and take possession of *Three Sisters* in our name."

Tremaine handed over the bill to Stairs as he continued.

"We cannot afford to have Mr. Jordan commit a rash act and abscond with our rightful property."

"Indeed not, sir. You may be sure I will not allow it," said the young man, his earnestness reflected in his face.

"Thou art from good stock, John," said Jonathan. "The Stayners and the Stairses are good people. We have always thought of thee as one of our own, have we not, brother John?" His brother nodded his agreement.

"I will strive to be worthy of your high regard, sirs," said Stairs, shaking the hand of each merchant before taking his leave.

TWO DAYS LATER, on the seventeenth of July, Stairs, Jordan, his family, and a small crew of three men set sail from Halifax. Bending over the chart table in *Three Sisters'* cabin, Tom Heath, the navigator, calculated their likely progress over the coming days. He hoped it would be a swift voyage, for he had a wife and two small children awaiting his return to Halifax. In truth, Heath had a bad feeling about the ship's owner, Ned Jordan, whom he had met only a few days previously. He did not like the Irishman's furtive gaze, the look of quiet desperation he sometimes caught crossing Jordan's dark face.

It had been a hard winter for Heath and other Halifax sailors, one of the coldest anyone could remember, punctuated by at least ten severe blizzards that had made going out in boats nearly impossible. Now that the good weather was here, Heath would take whatever work he could, even on a ship whose owner he instinctively distrusted.

"What ho, Tom?" The booming voice of Ben Matthews, *Three Sisters'* cheerful young deckhand, came roaring into the cabin, startling the navigator.

"Matthews—you rogue! What are you about?" he replied with some irritation, as Matthews bounded into the cabin, full of excitement.

"Quebec, Tom! We're bound for the Gaspé and a hundred glorious French girls! Huzzah!" He rubbed his hands together with delighted anticipation.

Heath looked disgusted, then smirked. "Steady, boy. There are a hundred sailors like yourself all converging on Gaspé even as we are speaking, all intent on getting a leg over a French girl, all destined for disappointment—the last time I was there, the only girls to be seen were either married or in convents."

Matthews was undaunted.

"Hogwash! That was a hundred years ago—those married women have since had time to breed daughters longing to be swept off their feet and onto their backs by a jolly Bluenose like myself!"

Heath could not help but smile at Matthews' enthusiastic brashness. Now in his thirties, Heath could well remember what it had been like to be a nineteen-year-old sailor on his first cruise, the heady sense of being away from home for the first time. Strong discipline would have to be applied to keep Matthews in line, just as it had been for Heath.

"Very well, very well, Matthews—have you finished scrubbing the foredeck?" asked Heath with a frown.

Matthews looked guilty.

"Not quite yet."

"Well? What are you waiting for? The deck will not clean itself! Do you want Jordan after you?"

With a grin, Matthews saluted Heath as crisply as if they had been in the British Navy, and then disappeared from the cabin.

STANDING AT THE SHIP'S WHEEL next to the captain, *Three Sisters'* thin and nervous-looking first mate John Kelly felt the summer breeze ruffle his hair and warm the skin on his pockmarked face, but barely noticed Matthews as he passed by. Like Jordan, Kelly was an Irishman; like Jordan, he never spoke of the reason for his departure from his native country. There was something unsettling about Kelly's vacant stare, although he performed his duties as a seaman competently enough. Stairs reflected that the mate had the kind of beaten-dog look that bespoke an unhappy childhood.

Calling out a greeting to Stairs and Kelly in his usual cheerful manner, Matthews caused the first mate to start as though he had received an electric shock. He cursed savagely at the deckhand and told him to get back to work or he would be lashed. Matthews hurried away. The captain stared at Kelly in bewilderment.

"Why, what ails you, man?" he asked. "He was merely offering you a good morning."

"He startled me, sir," said Kelly with a shrug. "He should be about his business and not disturbing other men's work with his trifles."

"You needn't be so hard on the lad in future, Kelly," said Stairs. "It is early in the journey, and I have no desire to create bad feeling among the crew."

"With all due respect, sir," said Kelly, "acting pert is but a step away from insubordination in my book. Deckhands need to know their place—and that ain't starting conversations with their superiors."

Stairs looked at Kelly with amazement. The mate was at least ten years older than Stairs, but he was not the captain of this ship! Stairs would not be talked back to while he was master. He spoke in measured tones, controlling the anger he felt flaring up in his chest.

"That is quite enough, Mr. Kelly. If I want your advice on how to run a ship, I shall ask for it."

Kelly shrugged dismissively. Stairs was outraged.

He sputtered, "If you do not accept my command, I will be happy to land you at Gaspé and find another mate. I shall also not hesitate to speak of your behaviour to the Tremaines and all the other merchants of Halifax upon our return. Is that what you want, Mr. Kelly?"

The mate said nothing, but stared off vacantly into space.

"I asked you a question, sir!"

"You may do as you see fit, captain," said the unrepentant Kelly, apparently unfazed by his master's reprimand.

"Very well. I see fit to put you on half rations for the remainder of the voyage. I shall be speaking to your employers within the month."

His face flushed, Stairs brushed angrily past Kelly, eager to quit his presence for a time.

Kelly waited until he heard the sound of the cabin door slamming shut, then burst into laughter. From the bow on the ship where he had been scanning the horizon, Jordan heard Kelly laughing, and walked back toward the stern to see what had so amused his countryman.

Bent over the wheel, his face scarlet and contorted, the first mate looked like he was choking in a spasm of laughter.

"What is it, Kelly?" asked Jordan.

Kelly could barely reply and seemed unaware of Jordan's presence.

"Cap'n John...thinks he's all grown up...giving orders. He puffs like an adder, but will soon be kicked like a puppy. Bastard! It's back to Sligo now I go..."

Jordan stared at Kelly in much the same way Stairs had done earlier. Could Kelly have been drinking, talking nonsense like this?

The hysterical laughter continued. On a sudden impulse, Jordan raised his hand and slapped Kelly hard across the cheek.

"Sober up, man!" he shouted. "I won't have a drunk steering my ship!"

Kelly's laughing fit abruptly ended, and he fixed his gaze on Jordan's frowning and concerned face.

"You have knocked some sense into me, sir," said the mate, solemnly. "I thank you for it, but I will not have you think I am a

drinking man. My Da drank himself to death before he was forty—
I do not wish to die in a similar way."

For a fleeting moment, Jordan thought of his own father, whose
efforts while his son had known him seemed to be concentrated in
much the same directions as Kelly's father's.

"If you weren't drinking, then what was that nonsense you were
raving on about just now?"

Kelly looked puzzled. "Oh dear, sir. I was just having my little
joke, to pass the time. I meant nothing by it."

Now Jordan was puzzled. "'Twas not a funny kind of joke, Kelly. You should be more careful with your words."

"That I will, good sir," said Kelly with a confiding wink.

"Did you say you came from Sligo?"

"That I did—I am a northerner, born and bred."

"What made you leave Ireland?"

Kelly looked cagey. "I might ask you the same thing, sir. But I
believe a man's privacy is his most prized possession and something
other men ought to respect."

Jordan nodded in agreement.

"Begging your pardon, sir," continued Kelly, in a tone no longer
confidential but entirely businesslike. "I have tasks to attend to and
must be at my work. Let us continue our conversation when we
both find ourselves unoccupied." He bowed slightly to Jordan,
who returned the bow. Jordan left Kelly at the wheel, whistling an
Irish jig, and returned to his watch at the other end of the ship.

THE DAY WAS CLEAR and breezy, the wind puffing out *Three Sisters'*
sails and propelling her quickly on her way. In three days, they had
cleared the Strait of Canso and entered the Gulf of St. Lawrence
on a northerly course toward Perce. With each passing mile, Jordan felt an increase in his dread. He knew there was no cod for
him at Johnson's; what's more, he felt sure that Stairs knew it too.
Though the two men were courteous to one another, Jordan felt
the younger man's contempt for him and his pity for Margaret
and the children, and was angered by it. They were on a fool's er-

rand, though of course no one said as much. Jordan increasingly felt himself a magnet for the disdain of the crew and of his family, Margaret especially. He saw how she gravitated toward the competent young captain, and resented his easy and courteous manner toward her. With bitterness, Jordan reflected that even his own children were turning against him. It was obvious that eight-year-old Neddy positively idolized Stairs, who made it a special point to teach the boy what he knew about sailing whenever he had the opportunity. Neddy soaked up the young captain's attention like a hungry sponge.

"How close are we to Perce, Captain Stairs?" the boy asked one morning five days into the voyage, as he did every morning since they left Halifax. To escape his father and his moods, Neddy often hung about the captain's cabin, hoping to be allowed inside. "Another fifty miles or so closer than the last time you asked me," replied Stairs with a friendly smile. Often, Stairs was preoccupied and spoke brusquely to the lad, but seeing how crushed Neddy was after turning him away, he had lately tried to be more kindly towards the unfortunate boy.

"May I look at the charts, Captain Stairs?" asked the boy eagerly, edging into the cabin, encouraged by his idol's friendly tone.

"Yes, boy—but only for a moment. Mr. Heath and I have important matters to discuss in private."

In fact, Stairs wished to speak to the more experienced navigator about John Kelly's insolent and sometimes erratic behaviour, which was taking its toll on the captain's peace of mind.

Pleased to be allowed into the captain's presence even for a few moments, Neddy climbed onto the stool at the chart table and studied the pencil marks made by Heath that showed the ship's position and how far it had travelled on each day of their voyage. Navigation fascinated Neddy, but being a captain like John Stairs was his dream.

While Neddy pored over the chart, completely absorbed, Stairs took Heath aside at the far end of the cabin, speaking in a low voice.

"I'd like to know what you make of the mate, Kelly. He and I have barely spoken since he displayed the grossest insolence to me the other day. I have told him his behaviour is reprehensible, and I will certainly not forget it when I am speaking to the Tremaines and others who might employ him in the future."

Heath nodded his head in agreement. "A strange fellow, that. And you certainly can't stand for him questioning your authority. Although I must say, it is not Kelly but Ned Jordan I have the most concern about."

Glancing over at the chart table where Jordan's son was seated, Stairs gestured to Heath to hold his peace a while.

"Neddy, I'm sorry but you will have to leave now. Mr. Heath and I are very busy today and need to work on that chart you are studying."

"Yes, sir." With reluctance, Neddy slid dejectedly off the stool and made for the cabin door.

"I will find you on deck presently and you shall have a look through my spyglass. Go find your sisters," said Stairs, by way of compensation. Neddy immediately brightened, and ran off to find Maggie and Sarah.

When he was gone, the two men resumed their conversation. "What concerns you about Jordan?"

"He keeps to himself a great deal—spends hours just standing at the bow, staring off into the distance. He is barely civil to me and Matthews. Kelly seems to be the only one he talks to."

Stairs nodded. "I have noticed that a friendship seems to have formed. They are both Irishmen—perhaps that accounts for it."

"Perhaps. But it seems they spend a great deal of time conversing while Kelly should be at his work. I don't like it."

"I have already spoken to Kelly about the matter. He agrees to whatever I say and obeys for a short while, then he seems to lapse into a world of his own where he cannot be reached."

Heath shook his head sadly. "A great shame it is, sir, about Kelly. I've heard it said around Halifax that he was a good sailor in his time. He certainly seems bright and competent enough. I confess

I wonder sometimes if he is in his right mind."

"I've had the thought myself," said Stairs. "We will have to keep a close eye on him—and on Jordan. I believe that he is leading us on a wild goose chase. Were I not in the Tremaines' debt for their many kindnesses to me when I was a child, I would not have undertaken this voyage."

Heath felt sorry for the young captain. He would not have wished to be in command on *Three Sisters* for all the tea in China.

Leaving the cabin, and Heath to his charts, Stairs kept his promise to Neddy and made sure the children each had a turn looking through the spyglass as they approached the magnificent pierced rock jutting up out of the ocean—the rock from which Perce had taken its name.

"You can see right through it!" cried Neddy excitedly to his sisters. "I'll bet you could swim through it, Captain Stairs!"

The young captain laughed heartily at the suggestion.

"I'm not much of a swimmer, Neddy. Maybe you will do it someday yourself."

AFTER THEY HAD DROPPED ANCHOR at Perce a few hours later, Stairs and Jordan took a dory ashore, leaving the small crew and the Jordan family behind. Stairs had thought of bringing Neddy and the men with them, but held back, sure of a humiliating revelation from Jordan that he felt no one else need witness.

"And where might we find Mr. Johnson's warehouse?" he inquired almost apologetically as they tied up the boat and walked along the wharf.

"It is but a short walk from here, but…" Jordan trailed off.

"Yes, Mr. Jordan?"

"I regret to say that any fish with which Mr. Johnson could supply us would have to be bought on credit against next season's catch. He owes me nothing. The most he could give us would be a hundred quintals."

Stairs pretended to look surprised. "One hundred? That is somewhat less than the two hundred you promised to the Tremaines."

Jordan nodded.

"In that case, Mr. Jordan, we will not trouble Mr. Johnson with a visit, but I will have to insist that you sign over your ownership of *Three Sisters* to my employers." From an inner pocket, he produced the bill of sale given to him by the Tremaines some days ago, and from another pocket, a quill and a small bottle of ink.

There was a pause in which Jordan fully digested the severity of his predicament. He felt a vast anger welling up within himself, directed at the world generally, and at the young captain in particular.

"You came prepared," he said bitterly, seizing the paper and signing away his ownership with one swift motion, the paper pressed against his left palm. He threw it down on the wharf. "There. It is done, and I am a ruined man. I hope you are well satisfied, Stairs."

Bending quickly to pick up the precious document, Stairs snapped at Jordan. "There is no need for spite, Mr. Jordan. You have brought this predicament fully upon yourself. Why did you lie about the cod and send me, the crew, and your family on a fool's errand?"

Seized with fury, Jordan grabbed Stairs by his collar and brought his face close to the younger man's, his black eyes burning in their sockets.

"See here, you son of a bitch. I may be destitute, but I'll not listen to your damned sermonizing about how I choose to live my life. It is no affair of yours. You can take the ship back to Halifax this day and leave me and my wife and children here. I curse the day I ever laid eyes on you and those pious Quaker bastards you work for."

He released Stairs and the two men rowed back to *Three Sisters* in stony silence.

When they were back on the ship, Stairs took a perturbed Margaret Jordan to one side as her husband threw their belongings angrily into a burlap sack in the cramped below-decks quarters and gently informed her that he had been forced to seize the ship in the name of Jordan's creditors.

"That is why your husband is angry with me and wishes to remain in Perce," said Stairs, reasonably.

Hearing this, Margaret dropped to her knees before him, crying, "Don't let him land us in this God-forsaken place, Captain Stairs, sir! Please let us return with you to Halifax—the people there at least speak English and I can take in washing for the navy and get Neddy apprenticed to one of the shops there. If we stay here, we'll starve. He's done it to us too many times before—moving us around the world like we were chattels on a cargo ship. Please, Captain Stairs, find it in your heart to bring us back with you..."

Her body convulsed with sobs, a piteous sound that stung the young captain's soul. He could not bear the sight of the unfortunate woman writhing before him. Bending down, he helped her to her feet. She clung to his arm for support.

"Please Mrs. Jordan. Do not abase yourself—your husband's predicament is not your fault."

Sensing Stairs' sympathy, Margaret dried her eyes, but did not let go of his arm.

"You have no idea, dear Captain John, what a tormented life I have led with that man. Dragged from pillar to post, me and my poor babies, these past ten years and more."

Stairs nodded sympathetically. "I really cannot imagine the trials you have endured, Mrs. Jordan."

There was an awkward pause as Stairs and Margaret stood immobile, looking at each other.

She spoke first.

"You are a handsome man, Captain Stairs. Always so well-dressed." She reached out and smoothed the collar of his jacket where her husband had grabbed it.

Stairs backed away slightly, clearly embarrassed. "Thank you, Mrs. Jordan...I have duties to attend to presently, but please consider yourself and your family my guests for our return voyage. I would not leave you and your children destitute."

She moved closer, far closer than was comfortable for him and spoke in a voice meant for his hearing only.

"Thank you, Captain. If there is any way that I can repay your kindness, you must tell me of it. At once. I wait only upon your pleasure." The final syllable brushed hotly against his ear. As she turned and walked away, he felt the brush of her fingers deliberate against him and it was as if someone had struck him across the knees with a heavy pipe. He watched her slow retreat as if in a daze, desiring and dreading her at the same time. He longed to possess a woman, but certainly not a married one and not before marriage. He thought of his betrothed, Catherine, far away in Halifax, and the promise they had made each other not long ago in her father's parlour. He thought of their honeymoon, seeing her uncovered for the first time. What would she think of his inexperience? What could Margaret Jordan teach him of the act of love? No—he must not even think it. He feared her husband's wrath more than God's, were he to act on this rash feeling. He would be her protector, not her lover. Stairs composed himself, and descended to his cabin where he splashed cold water on his face. He said sternly to himself, "I must act honourably, even if I am surrounded with dishonour. I will not disgrace myself and my family."

His mind made up, he left the cabin and busied himself with the ship.

Chapter 10

S tairs spent much of the next month locating and purchasing five hundred quintals of fish from local fishermen, as his employers had requested: one quintal representing 112 pounds, *Three Sisters* was soon laden with well over fifty thousand pounds of dried cod. Jordan took no part in the purchase or loading of the fish, spending much of his time silently brooding on the quarterdeck of the ship he had loved and lost. He had resigned himself quietly to a return to Halifax when Margaret had told him flatly that she would not stay in Quebec; with destitution hanging upon them all like a heavy wet cloak, it didn't matter now where they lived.

The loading of the fish having been completed, *Three Sisters* sailed with the tide on September 10, a warm and pleasant early fall afternoon that contrasted sharply with the atmosphere aboard the schooner. For three days, Jordan and Stairs had said no more than a handful of words to each other and avoided each other whenever possible—no easy task on a forty-five-foot ship. Stairs had to avoid Margaret Jordan, too, whose intentions were now obvious to everyone. The young captain felt equally ashamed of her attentions and of his consistent rebuffing of them. It was clear to Stairs that she desperately wanted to leave Jordan, whom she viewed as the instrument of her family's downfall. Could she truly think, though, that he, John Stairs, a sea captain with good prospects and of solid New England Protestant stock, would want to live with a penniless Irish-Catholic woman ten years his senior and her four brats, one of them a cripple? After a few days at sea, his coldness finally seemed to register with Margaret, who kept her distance thereafter.

From his quarters, Stairs could hear the Jordans engaging in terrible arguments, ones he half-expected would result in the deaths of both participants. He never intervened in these quarrels, of course, even when Margaret emerged the next morning badly bruised, with cuts on her face and arms. A man had no business involving himself in domestic disputes, and in his secret heart, he began to wish the Jordans would kill each other and rid the ship of its dreadful burden. That he might be one of the causes of such violent marital strife haunted Stairs.

For three days and nights, *Three Sisters* sailed in calm weather, crossing the Gulf once more and proceeding through the Strait of Canso. Just before noon on September 13, with a strong wind coming off the land, the captain sent Heath and Matthews forward to trim the sails. Stairs estimated that the ship must be about three miles east of Cape Canso, in the vicinity of White Head, but decided to take another sun reading to be certain they were well clear of land before making the turn to drop down the coast toward Halifax. He descended to his cabin for his sextant, followed shortly by Heath, who also wished to check their position.

Bent over the chart table examining their map, Stairs and Heath both looked up when a dark shadow passed by the skylight overhead, obscuring their view. At first, Stairs thought a storm cloud had crossed the face of the sun. But it was Ned Jordan peering down at them, his enraged face the only storm cloud on the horizon. At first, Stairs did not see the pistol that Jordan was holding, but when the desperate man raised his hand and fired at Stairs' head, the captain's immediate reaction was to duck instinctively away from the shot with a yell.

"Heath! He has a gun!"

There was a tremendous noise as the bullet shattered the glass. He felt something hot stinging his cheek—a piece of glass? Gunpowder? He did not have time to identify the sharp pain. Behind him, he heard a gurgling noise as Heath took the force of Jordan's bullet to the chest. Turning, Stairs saw blood pouring from the navigator's mouth as he toppled forward on his face whispering, "Oh my God, I am killed."

With a sharp shock of recognition, Stairs heard a voice of unknown origin speaking to him, "That bullet was for you, John."

Whose voice was it? Jordan's? His own?

Stunned, Stairs made a dive for the trunk where he kept his pistols: they were not there. The lock had been broken. When had Jordan taken them? How long had he been planning this bloody attack? Could Jordan have entered the cabin when Stairs and Neddy were looking through the spyglass at Perce? Again, Stairs did not have time to think. He felt raw and degraded. Then a murderous rage spread throughout his body—revenge was what he thirsted for. He saw blood-coloured fireworks exploding in the air in front of him. Mutiny! Is that what the Irish son of a whore thought this was?

He heard a second pistol shot on deck and Matthews' voice shrieking, "No! You shall not kill the captain! I will not let you kill him!"

The captain hurtled up the companionway, colliding with Jordan on the top step. The Irishman clutched Stairs' pistol in his right hand, a broad axe in his left. His black hair was standing on end as though he had been struck by lightning. The force of the collision sent Jordan sprawling backwards onto the deck and the axe tumbled out of his hand into the scuppers. Stairs fell upon him, intent on pulling the pistol out of his other hand. He felt the muzzle press into his chest and as if in a nightmare heard the click of flint on metal as Jordan pulled the trigger. Stairs thought he heard the Irishman whisper, "You are a dead man," at the same time as he formed the thought, "I am dead now, God help me." But no bullet penetrated him—the gun had not gone off. With a final desperate wrench and a guttural yelp, he pried the weapon free from Jordan's hand and threw it overboard. Panting and dazed, Stairs pleaded with his attacker.

"Jordan! Have you gone mad? Stop at once!"

But Jordan neither heard not heeded the captain, staggering to his feet and lunging for Stairs again.

"You shall not have my ship. You shall not have her," he repeated over and over in a frighteningly calm voice.

The two men locked arms in a sweaty, lumbering dance. Over Jordan's shoulder, Stairs could see the bleeding body of the deckhand, Ben Matthews; it was unclear if he had been killed outright by Jordan's bullet or if there was still life left in him.

While the two men were engaged in desperate combat, first mate John Kelly stood calmly at the wheel, incongruously keeping *Three Sisters* on course while chaos reigned aboard her. His pockmarked face was impassive, as though unaware of the mutiny that was taking place. Huddled in a corner of the small quarterdeck, spattered with the blood of deckhand Matthews, Neddy, Maggie, and Sarah Jordan could only stare in silent horror at the scene unfolding before their eyes. Margaret made no attempt to shield them from their father's murderous rampage; she could not see beyond her newly hatched hatred for the man whose rejection had slammed shut the door of her prison, depriving her and her children of what she saw as their last chance at freedom.

Jordan was heavier than Stairs, and clearly a more experienced fighter from his days on the streets of Carlow. His left fist glanced off Stairs' cheekbone, knocking him sideways. The captain knew he was overmatched, and called out to the mate for assistance.

"Kelly! Help me, man! For God's sake, Kelly—do you hear me?"

But Kelly made no move toward his beleaguered captain. Instead, whistling a lively Irish tune through broken teeth, he picked up the pistol Jordan had given him a few minutes earlier, and began polishing it thoughtfully with his shirt. Stairs could not believe his eyes. The Irishmen had formed a confederacy!

Now Margaret Jordan joined her husband in the fray. "Is it Kelly you want?" she sneered at the former object of her affections. "Very well—I'll give you Kelly!" Seizing a boat hook, she swung into the captain's abdomen, clearly intent on either disembowelling or castrating him, or both.

Her blow was checked by the hand of Matthews, who with his last remaining ounce of strength had pulled himself over to where the Jordans kept the captain within their deadly grip.

"Leave off, you scummy bitch," he mumbled, stabbing Margaret in the leg with his penknife. "Leave off the captain."

Unleashing a high-pitched scream of pain, Margaret dropped her hook, and with Matthews' knife still protruding from her thigh, rushed to the wheel, grabbed Kelly's pistol and fired at Matthews' head, missing him by inches.

"For God's sake, don't kill him!" cried Matthews in a final desperate act of protectiveness toward his young superior.

Seizing the broad axe from the scuppers, Jordan gave the deckhand his death with four crunching blows to the skull. Blood rained out like a burst water pipe, soaking the decks.

Maggie Jordan screamed once, then lost consciousness. The other children could only stare with horror, unable to move or speak.

Doubled over with pain, and with his attackers' attention drawn elsewhere for the moment, Stairs raced to the bow of the ship with the Jordans in pursuit.

"Give it to him, Ned!" cried Margaret with hysterical high-pitched laughter as she pressed the pistol into her husband's hand. "Kill the bastard!"

Stairs saw that he had no chance. Jordan cocked his gun and pointed it at the captain's head as Stairs' back touched the point of the bow. He bolted back toward the bloody quarterdeck, a trapped animal in a floating cage. His eye fell upon the booby-hatch, the sliding wooden panel covering the top of the cabin companionway—would it save him? In desperation, he grabbed the hatch, threw it into the ocean, and dove in after it. The cold seawater closed over his feet.

"The fool!" cried Ned Jordan. "He'd rather drown than be shot!" He pointed his pistol toward the wake of white bubbles where Stairs had entered the water.

Now Kelly held him back. "The sea will finish what you've begun, Jordan. Leave the poor man to his drowning."

"I will see the bastard die!" roared Jordan as *Three Sisters* pulled quickly away from the small figure in the water.

"You've done enough killing, man. He won't last twenty minutes in that water," reasoned Kelly. With reluctance, Jordan dropped his gun, watching as the small figure swam over to the floating hatch and pulled himself onto it before Jordan's view was obscured by rapidly drifting fog. Stairs' death would be slower than Jordan might wish, but no less satisfyingly final.

With the stiff southwest wind pushing them ever further down the coast of Nova Scotia towards the capital, Jordan, in command of his vessel once again, decided on a change of course. Abruptly, he yelled at Kelly, "Turn her around! We're bound for Newfoundland—the law will never find us there."

Kelly obeyed, spinning the wheel one hundred and eighty degrees. Neither he nor Jordan had ever been to Newfoundland, but both of them knew that its tiny coastal communities would make good hiding places while they waited out the storm Jordan was sure would follow the three murders and the taking of *Three Sisters*.

Seeing his son hunched down and shivering in a corner, a haunted look on his small face, Jordan now began to give orders.

"Get up and stop your bawling, you mamma's boy. Get the mop and swab down these decks. I don't want to see a spot of blood anywhere when you're finished. Now move!" Neddy jerked mechanically into action, too afraid of his father to refuse.

"Kelly!" yelled Jordan, moving swiftly to the place where Matthews had fallen. "Grab his feet and help me throw him over."

Heath's body was next; with the second splash, Jordan felt a sense of great elation. The evidence was now disposed of.

The tears on his son's cheeks as he slowly mopped up Matthews' blood infuriated Jordan, who had lost all sense of the cruelty he was inflicting on his own child.

"How do you like the life of a sailor now, boy?" he sneered. "I'll wager Captain Stairs didn't teach you this kind of lesson."

Dropping the mop, Neddy ran howling down the companionway steps and shut himself into the shattered cabin where shards of glass sparkled in pools of Heath's congealed blood. He screamed with horror. For the Jordan children, there was no escape now from the hell their lives had become.

As HE LAY ON HIS BACK on the hatch watching *Three Sisters* move farther and farther away, John Stairs felt a strange calm descend upon his soul. He knew that he would die of exposure in a matter of hours; even in September, when ocean temperatures were at their warmest, a man could only hold out for so long on the open waters of the North Atlantic. Stairs felt a certain grim satisfaction at having foiled Jordan's attempt to shoot him; he kept himself warm for a time by allowing his burning hatred for the Irishman and his wife to permeate his being.

As the hatch rose and sank on the waves, bearing Stairs with it, the young man fell into a kind of hypothermic trance, fantasizing about the capture of *Three Sisters* and the hanging of the Jordans and Kelly. An hour passed. The fog began to lift. Stairs felt sunshine burst down upon him, warming his back. Thoughts, fragments of thoughts rose up and subsided in his mind. An old fisherman's prayer: "Oh God, thy ocean is so large and my little boat so small." His mother's fevered face as she bid her eight-year-old son goodbye. Something from the Bible he remembered hearing as a fidgeting child in church, "When the sea shall give up its dead…"

He thought of all the men before him who had drowned in this ocean. Had they had time to feel this agony? What a short time he had been on earth and how much there was that he still longed to accomplish! Catherine—would she marry someone else when she learned that he had died? He felt tears prickle his eyes as his strength ebbed. He thought about rolling off his little raft, ending his life quickly, but fear held him back. Suicides were God's enemies; he wished to die with a clear conscience. He began to hallucinate, his body shuddering convulsively as the wind chilled him to the marrow of his bones: strange whales with human faces cresting beneath the hatch, sucking him into their great mouths through hairy swaths of baleen. A mermaid swimming beside the hatch, her long golden hair streaming out around her like the sun's corona, her great green tail fin tickling his hands and feet seductively.

"Woman..." he called out, delirious, "Take me down with you! I long to die in your arms..."

The womanfish bobbed like a curious seal for a few moments, showing him her pale breasts, their tempting raspberry-coloured nipples, then turned tail and dove beneath the heaving sea, beyond his reach.

As his breathing grew more laboured, he imagined he saw a schooner passing near him, close enough for him to hear the billowing of wind in sailcloth, the excited shouts of crewmen—"Look, boys! I believe he's been shipwrecked. Is that a hatch he's floating on?"

Another fantasy...Stairs knew he must be near the end. He was too weak even to turn his head away from the painful vision.

With a jerk, he felt himself himself lifted upwards by two strong seamen. They carried him to the warmth of a ship's cabin, where solicitous hands undressed him, laid him on a comfortable pallet, and piled him high with blankets.

"Give him rum, boys...no, brandy," said a deep voice with a broad New England accent.

It was not a dream! He had been rescued.

Chapter 11

With her graceful lines and neat, well-scrubbed appearance, the fishing schooner *Eliza* was the delight of her master, Levi Stoddard, who hailed from the little town of Hingham, just south of Boston, Massachusetts. To John Stairs, she was nothing less than a miracle—he vowed that if God ever blessed him with a daughter, she should be called Eliza, too.

"That's her, sir—that must be her—it's *Three Sisters*! She's bearing east by northeast—Jordan must be taking her to Newfoundland! We'll have no trouble catching her," said Stairs with excitement. Now that he had been plucked from the jaws of death, his thoughts were bent on pursuing Ned Jordan and taking possession of the stolen ship once more.

Stoddard looked doubtful. "She's a good piece off, Mr. Stairs. Doubtful if we could catch up to her before nightfall."

"But, my dear sir—I have an obligation to my employers to protect their property. With your kind assistance, I can fulfill that obligation, and see those mutinous bastards hanged into the bargain."

Stoddard lowered his glass, and looked Stairs squarely in the eye.

"That may be so, Mr. Stairs, but the plain facts are these: I have a duty to protect this ship and her crew from harm. From what you have told me about Jordan, I have grave reservations about the safety of my men, were we to attempt to board your ship. Also, if anything were to happen to my ship, the underwriters would not pay the insurance."

Stairs looked impatient, though he grudgingly had to admit Stoddard was simply being prudent. He spoke with a pleading tone in his voice.

"But there are six of us, and only two of them—we could easily overcome them with the odds so much in our favour!"

"You say Jordan still carries a gun?"

Stairs nodded grimly.

"I cannot endanger the lives of my men against an armed and desperate lunatic. I am sorry, Mr. Stairs. I cannot imagine what horrors you have had to endure at the hands of this Jordan, but I am captain here, and I have made up my mind. We will not be chasing any damned schooner all the way to Newfoundland."

Anger momentarily welled up in Stairs' chest; he did not like being in a subordinate position aboard any ship, even one that had lately saved his life.

"In that case, sir," he said in a clipped voice. "I would be greatly obliged if you would take me to Halifax so I can inform the authorities of what has taken place and have one of our ships sent out to apprehend her."

An apologetic look crossed Stoddard's narrow, weatherbeaten face.

"Mr. Stairs, I am sorry to have to disappoint you a second time, but I will not be able to land you in Halifax."

Stairs looked stunned. "May I ask why not, sir?"

"On our voyage out of Hingham some weeks ago, we tried to put in at Halifax for fresh supplies when we were set upon by the British cruiser *Bream*. We were boarded and our best sailor was impressed. Damn Brits think they have a right to any seaman, whether he's a citizen of the Crown or not. Our bo'sun, Rich Davidson, became an American citizen just after we gained our independence and has been living in Boston for years, but try to tell that to a Limey recruiting sergeant!"

Stoddard looked disgusted, and once again, Stairs felt a surge of resentment toward the American captain. Like many Nova Scotians, Stairs had strong ancestral ties to New England, but his loyalties were firmly with the King and Mother England. Stairs' ships would always fly the Red Ensign, not the Stars and Garters, nor the irksome flag directly beneath it that read, "God and Sailors' Rights." In the good old British Navy tradition, sailors had no rights—they lived to be beaten and whipped into a cowed, disciplined fighting machine, as Stairs himself could well attest. Though he had silently cursed the British navy many and many a time aboard *Hussar*, he would not hear an American upstart deride the home country in such a way. Duty! What would the Yankees know of that? Where had they been when Nelson was shot at Trafalgar? That Stoddard might be justified in his views on illegal impressment did not enter Stairs' mind.

Unable to conceal his extreme annoyance any further, the young man stiffly excused himself and retired below decks, seething silently in his bunk as *Three Sisters* pulled farther and farther away.

A FEW DAYS LATER, Captain Stoddard made an attempt to land his passenger at Cape Sable on the southwestern shore of Nova Scotia, but gale-force winds made the approach unwise, and Stoddard soon gave up the endeavour. He would have to bring Stairs back to *Eliza*'s home port of Hingham, and from there, the young man could shift for himself.

Nine days after being forced to jump into the Atlantic, Stairs sat in the office of W.S. Skinner, the British consul in Boston, and related his amazing tale. Skinner shook his head in disbelief at Stairs' story, scarcely believing that the young man could have survived his ordeal. Sensing the older man's doubt, Stairs said, "If you don't believe me, sir, talk to Levi Stoddard and his men—they'll tell you what a close shave I had. Better yet, send a cruiser out this very day to hunt down Jordan and Kelly: if they deny their actions, they are perjurers as well as murderers!"

Skinner lost no time in circulating the particulars of Stairs' story, along with a thorough physical description of *Three Sisters* and Ned Jordan, to every customs collector on the Atlantic seaboard, authorizing the immediate arrest of Jordan and Kelly for piracy and murder. News of the outrage reached Stairs' home province in early October, where, with the perpetrators still at large, a bounty of one hundred pounds sterling was placed on Ned Jordan's head by Governor George Prevost.

On the morning of October 10, John Tremaine was on his way to work when he was startled by the cries of the newsboy on the corner of Morris and Water streets:

"Mutiny on the *Three Sisters*! Captain Stairs thrown overboard! Jordan still at large!" Jumping from his carriage before thinking to tell the driver to stop, Tremaine tumbled precipitately into the street, made muddy and treacherous to pedestrians by heavy autumn rains.

"What was thy news of *Three Sisters*, lad?" he demanded of the now equally startled newsboy.

"Mutiny, sir," piped the child, "Jordan the pirate has killed two of her crew and is still at large."

The lanky merchant's mouth fell open.

"You may read all the particulars in the *Gazette*, sir," the newsboy gently reminded him. "Hot off the press this morning."

"Yes, yes—" said Tremaine, rummaging in his pockets for change.

"Thank you, sir. Good day to you. Mutiny aboard *Three Sisters*! Jordan the pirate still at large!" The newsboy ended the conversation in his professional voice, several decibels louder than he had begun it.

Standing on the street corner, Tremaine felt horror grip him as he delved into the story that blanketed the pages of the *Royal Gazette*:

From our correspondent:
Hingham, Sept 22, 1809: The Schooner Eliza, *Stoddard, master, has just arrived at this port. He picked up at sea Capt. John Stairs, who gives the following particulars respecting himself.*

"On the 13ᵗʰ September, 1809, the schooner Three Sisters *was risen upon by a passenger by the name of Edward Jordan, about three miles to the westward of Cape Canso, and about four miles southward of the land; he shot two of my crew and I was forced to jump overboard to save my life, and was very fortunately picked up by Captain Levi Stoddard of the schooner* Eliza *of Hingham.* Three Sisters *belongs to Messrs. Jonathan and John Tremaine of Halifax. —John Stairs."*

We at the Royal Gazette *hope our fellow Printers in neighbouring Provinces, indeed, in all parts of the world, will give publicity to Capt. Stairs' report, and the following necessary particulars—they may lead to the apprehension of the perpetrators.*

A detailed description of Jordan's and Kelly's age, height and colouring, as well as the dimensions of the ship they were sailing in, followed Stairs' disturbing testimony.

Tremaine shuddered as he read the long article, and had an especially odd feeling at seeing his name in print in connection with so sordid a business. He felt great shame at allowing himself to be taken in by Jordan's tale of woe, and dreaded showing the paper to his brother, who was sure to be incensed.

The merchant continued his journey on foot, his mind in a turmoil. Jordan had to be caught, that much was evident. The ship and its cargo—not to mention the lives Jordan had taken—were too valuable. There would be a trial, and most certainly a hanging. Tremaine felt terribly uneasy at this prospect. There had been far too many hangings in Halifax of late, in his opinion. Just last month, on September 18, four men were gibbeted on Maugher's Beach at MacNab's Island for their part in a mutiny aboard HMS *Columbine*, a Halifax-based warship patrolling the waters near St. Andrews, New Brunswick. It was rumoured that some of the impressed men had tried to protest their ill treatment aboard *Colum-*

bine by deserting to the United States, whose border lay but sixty miles south of their position, and whose navy paid its sailors three times more than its British counterpart. When *Columbine's* officers had tried to stop the would-be deserters, violence had broken out on board. Twenty-three men had been captured and court-marshalled and twelve condemned to death or exile in New South Wales. Now, the bodies of four of the *Columbines* hung rotting in chains at the entrance to the harbour like many a sailor before them, a bitter fourfold warning to potentially like-minded sailors aboard His Majesty's warships.

A peace-loving man, John Tremaine had grown profoundly weary of the ceaseless round of impressments and hangings that went along with living in a British seaport. Halifax had always been a brutal town, especially in times of war, and everyone knew war was soon coming, this time with the United States. Their last president, Jefferson, had just a short time ago lifted his country's embargo on the import and export of British goods, his angry response to Britain's boarding and pressing of "British" subjects aboard American ships. The repercussions of Jefferson's punitive action were keenly felt in Halifax, which had since its founding enjoyed a healthy trade with its southern neighbour. Though business had been good lately, with a new and belligerent president, James Madison, now in office, Tremaine and other merchants feared a naval war with the States, which would further cripple their ability to trade. The Tremaines could ill afford to lose *Three Sisters*, for any reason.

Sitting down at his desk, John hurriedly penned the notice he knew his brother would certainly insist upon.

The subscribers wish to inform the reading public that a reward of one hundred dollars is hereby offered for the apprehension of Ned Jordan and John Kelly in addition to the one hundred pounds offered by His Excellency, Sir George Prevost in his recent proclamation. The subscribers are the owners of the schooner Three Sisters, *now at large, and of her valuable cargo of fish. —Jonathan and John Tremaine, merchants of Water Street, Halifax.*

Having addressed the letter to the publisher of the *Gazette*, Tremaine now turned his mind to the matter of his unfortunate employee, John Stairs. The paper mentioned nothing of Stairs' immediate plans, though Tremaine surmised he would return to Halifax on the next available vessel. Would the young captain be able to shed any light on the whereabouts of *Three Sisters*? Had he been injured in his terrible ordeal? Tremaine picked up the paper again and scanned the columns for details. No, there was no word of any injury to Stairs.

The next letter that Tremaine set about writing was addressed to Captain Stoddard, by whose kindly intervention the young man had been saved. After expressing his most sincere thanks to the captain, he carefully folded a twenty-dollar bill between the pages of his letter and addressed the envelope simply, "Capt. Stoddard, Hingham, Mass." He sealed the envelope with a healthy gob of wax. The good captain would find no use for British pounds in Massachusetts these days, though in Halifax, both pounds and dollars were common currency.

His final letter of the morning was addressed to John Stayner, expressing his concern for Stayner's adopted son and nephew, and his certainty that the wrongdoers would be brought swiftly to justice. He felt the latter was the proper thing to say under the circumstances, although his own thirst for vengeance had been completely quenched in a tide of sadness for the lamentable state of the world.

Chapter 12

October 1809, Bay of Bulls, Newfoundland—

Ned Jordan sat slumped over a mug of whisky at a dirty tavern just a few miles away from St. John's, unable to concentrate on even the smallest detail of his current situation.

How he and Kelly had managed to get the ship this far was beyond him: of the harrowing voyage from Canso to Newfoundland, Jordan could remember only bits and pieces. The day after Stairs had jumped overboard, Kelly had begun having angry conversations with himself, scaring the children, who overheard him.

"Turn back, you bastard! The captain needs your help—see how he reaches for your hand even as the sea is about to swallow him up!" he yelled in a deep voice, leaning so far over the port railing the children were sure he would fall over.

Jerking back suddenly, Kelly now spoke in a trembling falsetto, "Tut, tut, Kelly—you are a fool. Stairs is dead; he cannot harm you now. You know we never liked him. He was an arrogant puppy."

"Confess your deed before you go to Hell," warned Kelly's strong voice.

"Run away where no one will find you!" advised his weak voice.

"Can he be two people at once?" whispered Maggie to her brother as they huddled together out of Kelly's earshot.

"Of course not," Neddy hissed. "He's gone mad, just like Da and Ma."

"Da is not mad!" Maggie shot back, defensively. "He had too much to drink—worrying about us has made him sick. He is not a bad man."

"Yes he is," said Neddy fiercely. "And Ma is bad too. They killed two men and left Captain Stairs to drown. They both should be hanged, like the man on McNab's Island."

Maggie rocked back and forth, a terrible feeling of helplessness gripping her. She would not, could not believe her parents were evil, especially her beloved Da. "If they get hanged, who will take care of us?" she asked, tears rolling down her cheeks.

Neddy shrugged. "No one. We must take care of ourselves now."

The nine-year-old did not know how closely his words resembled those his father had spoken to himself almost thirty years ago when he had run away from Carlow.

While the children anxiously watched Kelly's raving on the deck of *Three Sisters*, their father emerged from the cabin, a deep frown on his face and dark circles beneath his eyes. Maggie longed to run to him and be comforted, as in the old days, but sensed the danger he represented now. Would he kill her, too, like those poor sailors? Would she have to jump overboard like Captain Stairs?

"Damn you, Kelly—what are you on about now? Can't a man have any peace and quiet without being disturbed by your madness?"

"Ah, Jordan, we are lost! Lost, I tell you!" shouted Kelly, pulling a knife from his boot and holding it to his own throat. "Let us finish it here, end our lives now. Why wait for the gallows?"

Maggie tried to scream, but her brother clamped his hand over her mouth to stop the sound.

With a curse, Jordan knocked the knife from Kelly's hand, sending it clattering to the deck.

"We'll have no more of that. I mean to get us to Newfoundland, and you are the better navigator of us two."

Kelly stared at Jordan, tears pouring down his face. "I cannot help you now, Jordan. I am a dead man."

Jordan sneered at Kelly. "You can slit your own throat once we get to Bay of Bulls, but you must help me bring the ship safely there first. If you try any foolishness before then, you will be visited in Hell by the souls of my poor children—they will haunt you for eternity."

Maggie and Neddy shivered at these words.

With great difficulty, Jordan finally convinced Kelly to come to the cabin and help him plot a course to the eastern coast of Newfoundland. He then gave Neddy instructions never to let Kelly out of his sight and to fetch him immediately if he caught the mate making preparations for suicide.

"If he kills himself, I shall hold you responsible," he told his son, whose face went pale.

The next day, Jordan spotted land to the northeast, and a few days after that, Kelly announced that they were approaching the entrance to Bay of Bulls.

It was early morning when they dropped anchor, and the village had not yet come to life.

Kelly rowed the dory while Jordan kept his face hidden under the collar of his threadbare coat. Even with no one around, he feared being recognized.

They had barely pulled up alongside the wharf when Kelly suddenly dropped his oars and bolted out of the boat, running hard.

"Kelly! Come back!" shouted Jordan, but it was no use. Kelly was gone.

His DISAPPEARANCE was the least of Jordan's worries. Since his arrival in Bay of Bulls, he had passed under the name of Edward Tremaine, but news of the *Three Sisters'* disappearance would soon reach even this remote outport, and Jordan knew it. He quickly engaged Patrick Power, a fellow Irishman with navigation skills acquired during years of fishing off the coast of Newfoundland, telling him he was a Limerick merchant returning to Ireland to fetch supplies for the spring fishing season on the Grand Banks. The two men agreed that Power should receive eleven pounds a month until he was discharged. Power harboured misgivings about his new employer; this

Tremaine fellow drank heavily and had a violent temper when in his cups. Just before they were to leave Newfoundland, Power overheard Jordan and his wife in a terrible argument on board the ship.

"You are a black-hearted murderer, Ned Jordan!" he heard the woman scream from the cabin. "You threaten me one more time and I'll tell the justice of the peace what I know—I'll see you hanged yet!"

"Shut your mouth!" replied the angered husband. "What's to stop me from smashing your skull in, tell me that?"

"I'm the mother of your children, you blackguard, though I curse the day I ever brought you to my bed!"

There was a crash as of smashing crockery, and a scream.

"You'd spread your legs to the first man came along—you'd have bedded Stairs, but he wouldn't have you, you fawning bitch."

The dispute raged on, and Power tried to block it out, though only a thin wall separated his cramped sleeping quarters from the fighting couple's. He was used to fighting—his parents had fought every day of their married lives—and he knew that women were prone to exaggeration when their blood was up, but what of this business of Mr. Tremaine being a murderer—for that matter, his not being Mr. Tremaine at all but one Ned Jordan? Had his wife been drinking? Power himself had once punched someone so hard in a drunken brawl that the man had died the next day, but that had been years ago, up north, and the man was only an Indian so no one had made much of it. Power had moved to another town and taken a different name for a while in case things got hot for him, but they never did. No, this business sounded much more serious. What could Power do now to get out of his contract with Tremaine, or Jordan, or whatever the man's name was? Should he slip away tonight while they were still hard at it in the cabin?

"Power!" Jordan suddenly bellowed from his quarters. "Come in here at once!"

Power pushed open the door to the cabin and saw Margaret Jordan bruised and bleeding on the floor. She was not moving.

"I think I've killed her," said Jordan. "And you're my witness.

She fell down the companionway stairs, didn't she, Power? If anyone asks." His dark eyes gleamed with menace; Power was certain that the man had gone mad.

Before he could answer, Margaret made a soft moaning sound, twitching slightly.

Jordan looked rather disappointed at these signs of life in his spouse.

"Oh well, no matter now," he grinned at Power, then stepped over his wife on his way to the door. "I need some air. Get up off the floor, woman, and see to your children. We ship out tomorrow morning."

Power said nothing. Margaret wept silently on the cabin floor. He reached down and offered her a hand. She did not accept it, seemingly drained of the energy required to stand upright. She spoke in a thin voice that seemed to belong to a ghost: "You do not know the life I lead with that man. I know that he will kill me before we reach Ireland. He keeps two pistols beneath our berth and threatens to shoot me every night."

"Why?" asked Power. "What have you done for him to use you so?"

"If I tell you, he will certainly kill me and leave our children orphans, for he will hang for it. I know the kind of man he is."

With that, Margaret Jordan slowly and with great pain raised herself off the floor and limped to her berth where, oblivious or indifferent to Power's presence, she removed her clothing and lay down to sleep. Transfixed by the number of bruises and abrasions she revealed in her undressing, Power stood motionless for a moment. Then, embarrassed, he backed out of the cabin and returned to his own quarters, with fresh doubts crowding his mind. He could not entertain them for long, however, for the voyage on *Three Sisters* meant much-needed money to Power.

IN THE NEXT FEW DAYS, Jordan managed to assemble a skeleton crew of two more men: John Pigot, a fisherman from Fortune Bay, and a seaman named William Crew. All of them were concerned by

Jordan's drinking and the vague answers he gave them as to their date of departure. Pigot was especially worried about Jordan's capricious attitude towards their eventual destination: he had originally agreed to ship with Jordan to Halifax, then to Ireland, but now Jordan seemed bent on sailing directly for Ireland, bypassing the Nova Scotia capital altogether.

The day he was hired by Jordan, with Power and Crew on shore filling casks of water for the voyage, Pigot had descended to the ship's hold to inspect her cargo and had found it all in disarray—the barrels of salt cod Stairs had bought in Quebec were now rolling loose from one end of the hold to the other, some split open, and their contents scattered about. Among the stiff, grey bodies of the fish, Pigot had detected the silver glint of steel and had pulled out a rifle from beneath the pile. Picking up the weapon, he felt sweat prickling the back of his neck. Why would someone hide a gun here? Such a powerful weapon ought surely to be secured in a chest above decks, he thought.

Sensing danger, Pigot climbed out of the hold and swiftly informed his employer that he would not sail on *Three Sisters* after all.

"Why not?" glowered Jordan, already in his cups at this early hour of the morning.

"Because I do not desire to go," replied Pigot defiantly.

Jordan stared at him for several seconds, then laughed heartily.

"Well, lad, it seems you're out of luck. You signed a contract, see—and until we get to Ireland, you owe me your services."

Pigot said nothing, but impulsively made for the starboard railing and prepared to drop over into the boat that was tied to her side.

Jordan seized him by the arm.

"No you don't, you bastard. You try going back to Bay of Bulls, I'll inform the customs master that you broke your contract. You'll be tied to the flagstaff and have the hide whipped off your back this very day!"

Anger flared up in Pigot's chest. "Take your hands off me! Power's told me of your drinking and how you serve your wife—and now I've seen for myself the mess you keep the ship in. This here's a runaway ship if ever I saw one—and I'll tell the customs man that, too."

Jordan pulled a pistol from his jacket pocket and pointed it at Pigot's head.

"No you won't, lad. Now step away from the side, and go down and see to the fish. I expect to see it well in order by the time I return, or there'll be hell to pay, d'you mark me?"

Terrified, Pigot nodded.

Later, packing the salt fish back into barrels in the hold, he muttered to himself, "That's what we are now, I warrant—fish in a barrel."

ON CREW AND POWER'S RETURN, *Three Sisters* finally left Bay of Bulls for the open ocean. Margaret Jordan was too weak to rise from her berth and watch the retreating granite headlands behind them; all four children had joined her in the cabin, and they huddled together in mute terror like beaten animals.

Scanning the horizon just after their departure, Jordan could see a worrisome speck of sail that seemed to grow larger and larger—or was it just his imagination? Pulling out the spyglass that had once belonged to John Stairs, he trained the instrument on the speck. It was, indeed, a ship—a schooner—and flying the red ensign. Cold sweat began to form under Jordan's collar, even in the crisp sea breeze. Could she be coming for him? Jordan shook off the idea with vehemence. Maybe the schooner was short of men and was chasing the *Three Sisters* to impress its crew, forcing her back to Bay of Bulls for the winter. That was the answer, Jordan told himself, unconvincingly. His thoughts were a choir of cacophonous voices all speaking at once: some frantic and high-pitched, others low and soothing. A sonorous voice, deep and insistent, spoke to him like the chorus of a Greek tragedy: "They have come, Jordan. They have come for you at last."

He watched the ship approach steadily, even as *Three Sisters* lumbered along like the heavy-laden merchant vessel she was. There was no question of outrunning the swift-pacing schooner, of that much Jordan was certain. They would have to feign innocence and hope for the best.

Climbing down from the quarterdeck, Jordan called for his crew. He tried to sound calm as he spoke to them, his jaw clenched.

"There's a ship bearing down on us; they are like to impress the three of you and send us back to port directly. That's all—go back to your posts."

Turning back toward the schooner that was steadily gaining on *Three Sisters*, Jordan crossed himself, speaking through suppressed tears, "The Lord have mercy on me! What will my poor children do?"

The men watched in silence over the next several hours as the British ship gained ground on *Three Sisters*, relief growing in them as steadily as the mounting fear within Jordan.

When the schooner came within range of its quarry, its crew fired a shot across the bow from its four-pound carronade as a warning to *Three Sisters* to heave-to. Already, Jordan's ship was travelling slowly, and the schooner was soon close enough for the crew of *Three Sisters* to see the uniforms of the men on its decks.

Soon they were addressed by the schooner's captain, his voice amplified by a speaking-trumpet.

"Edward Jordan, John Kelly and all those aboard *Three Sisters*: this is the captain of *Cuttle* speaking. Heave-to and prepare to be boarded!"

"Keep calm, lads," said Jordan to his crew. "I'll handle this."

Shouting at the top of his lungs, Jordan replied, "There is no one by that name aboard this ship—I am John Stairs, captain of *Three Sisters*, bound for Halifax."

"Edward Jordan and John Kelly, prepare to be boarded!" repeated the captain as a party of marines boarded one of the ship's boats and rowed the short distance to *Three Sisters*, their weapons close at hand, their faces grim and wary. They were soon climbing aboard the unfortunate vessel.

The captain boarded last, a look of triumph in his eyes. The man standing before him fit the newspaper description to the letter: dark eyes, black hair and beard, a strangely innocent expression. After hearing about Jordan's crimes, the men had been expecting a devil. They were surprised, almost disappointed, to find only a man.

"That's him, lads," said the captain, signaling to his burly midshipman. "That's Jordan, the pirate."

In seconds, three young *Cuttle* sailors had seized Jordan and pinned his arms behind his back while a midshipman handcuffed his prisoner. Jordan made no attempt to resist his captors. He knew that his long journey was rapidly coming to an end.

Descending below decks, a small party of men found Margaret Jordan and her children curled together in their berth, as they had been for much of the voyage. Seizing Margaret roughly by the wrist, a marine pulled her up the companionway to where the captain stood impassively. She did not put up any resistance, too weak even to scream. Her two younger children clung terrified to her skirts as she was hauled before her captor, her head bowed in silent submission.

"I found her, sir—the little witch what gave Captain Stairs his blows about the head with the boathook."

"Very good, Mr. Young. Where are the other children? I was told there were four."

"Still below, sir—I'll fetch 'em."

By the time the young marine had returned with Maggie and Neddy, their parents were already in the *Cuttle*'s boat, their hands bound.

The captain turned now to Power, Pigot, and Crew, who had stood by in amazement while the Jordans were placed under arrest.

"As for you," he said sharply to the three hapless seamen, "I don't know which one of you is John Kelly; I was given no intelligence as to any other of Jordan's accomplices—but I'll find out soon enough."

"Kelly, sir?" said Pigot, perplexed. "None of us goes by that name. These two men and I are the only crew of this wretched ship."

"What are your names?" asked the captain, suspiciously.

"I'm Pigot, and these here are Bill Crew and Pat Power," said the seaman, indicating his two mates.

The captain turned to his midshipman. "Take these men with

you in the boat. Until we find out which one of 'em is lying, I don't want them out of my sight."

"We ain't lying, sir!" protested Power. "We was hired on just days ago by the man you arrested," he gestured to Jordan. "What's he done?"

"He's nothing but a damned pirate!" said the midshipman, looking at Jordan with disgust.

"He killed two men on this ship."

The three seaman looked truly appalled by this knowledge.

"We had no idea, sir," stammered Pigot, horrified. "He told us a story about being a Limerick merchant. We had nothing to do with any piracy!"

"We'll see about that," said the captain, gesturing to the midshipman, who tied their hands and shoved them into the boat along with the Jordans.

As the captain gave orders for several of *Cuttle*'s twenty-man crew to stay aboard *Three Sisters* and see her brought back to Halifax, the midshipman's party rowed the prisoners back to the schooner. Jordan appeared oblivious to his surroundings.

"My poor Maggie," he said, tears streaming down his face. "I had hopes, such fine hopes once. "

JOHN KELLY RAN through the woods, splashing through streams and brackish water, his face bleeding where it had been scourged by the boughs of hemlock and spruce as he whipped past. Panic filled his being as he heard voice and hoofbeats close behind him.

"We've got you, Kelly—you cannot escape."

He was a wounded animal pursued by hounds, but the chase would soon be over: Kelly could see an opening in the trees ahead and the drop of land down to the merciless ocean below. He knew he was trapped.

Ever since quitting *Three Sisters*, a ship he viewed as cursed, he had kept to himself as far as was possible in a village the size of Bay of Bulls while he desperately awaited the arrival of a ship, any ship, that would return him to Ireland, where he might disappear into the slums of Dublin or Cork and be forgotten. But it was Lieutenant Cartwright of the Nova Scotia Regiment who had come instead, accompanied by a search party and armed with a warrant for his and Jordan's arrests, and Kelly knew his luck had run out. With his description on the front page of every newspaper from London to New York, the net soon closed around the Irishman.

Approaching the cliff, Kelly stopped running, bending low over his knees and gulping the cold air. Cartwright's search party closed in, the lieutenant mounted on a chestnut mare who whinnied almost sympathetically at Kelly. Cartwright dismounted, surveying his quarry. His voice, roughened by tobacco, stung Kelly's ears.

"John Kelly, you are under arrest on charges of piracy and mutiny on the high seas."

Seeing three soldiers approaching him, Kelly drew his knife and held it to his own throat.

"Stay back! I will put an end to myself here and spare His Majesty the expense of a trial. I wish to live no longer."

As Kelly pressed the blade to his throat, slicing into the skin, four of Cartwright's men lunged toward him, knocking the weapon from his hand. They pulled him expertly to the ground and held him there, while Kelly Gasped with sobs and twisted like a fish pulled from the water. The lieutenant stood over him, a disapproving look on his face.

"Now, now—we'll have none of that, Mr. Kelly. I have been requested to bring you to Halifax alive to stand trial, and alive you shall return with me. Wilkinson! Search the prisoner for other weapons."

Pulling the now-limp Kelly to his feet, a soldier turned out every pocket but could find no other weapons.

"Please you, sir," pleaded Kelly, "if you will not allow me to do it, will you not kill me yourself, here? I am haunted by the curse of *Three Sisters*. Truly, I have no wish to live beyond this day." Tears streamed down his face as he spoke.

The soldiers looked at each other uncomfortably.

"You heard me, Kelly," said Cartwright, apparently unperturbed.

"You shall return to Halifax to stand trial— afterwards, perhaps the court shall grant you your wish." He smirked. To his men, the lieutenant called out briskly, "Bind his hands and feet. Leave him enough rope to walk."

They marched the pinioned Kelly back to the village in silence. It was afternoon and Mrs. Henderson was bringing in laundry from the windy clothesline in her yard. The young woman stared at the procession that came out of the woods and marched slowly toward the harbour where a ship awaited them. The spindly limbs of the prisoner were bound, and he shuffled along at a slow pace as a consequence. His face was deathly white and he bled from a cut at his throat. Mrs. Henderson was close enough to the road to see the tears staining his downcast face, which was pitted with smallpox, and she felt a pang of sympathy for a man so beset. Who was he and what had he done to deserve this shameful treatment?

A soldier in the procession, impatient with his captive's foot-dragging, gave the unfortunate man a shove, knocking him side-ways and nearly toppling him.

"Damn you, Kelly—look alive, will you?" he cursed.

Mrs. Henderson felt a cold shiver pass along her spine. Was this John Kelly, the infamous pirate whose crimes she and her neigh-bours had very lately heard about? Was this the same man who had stood by while two crewmen were killed and their captain forced to jump overboard? The sympathy she had felt for the prisoner melted like a spring snowfall and was replaced with a strong sense of out-rage. Her husband, like most of the men in the village, earned his livelihood as a fisherman; his job was dangerous enough without having to worry about pistol-wielding pirates boarding his ship and seizing its cargo. How grateful she was now to the men who had captured one such evildoer!

Seizing a handkerchief from her basket, she ran out to the side of the road and waved it vigorously at the soldiers as they passed.

Lieutenant Cartwright tipped his hat and called out "Afternoon, ma'am."

"God bless you, sir, you gots one of 'em! I could kiss you!"

Cartwright smiled, lifting his hand to signal a pause in the march. His men smirked—they knew he rarely passed up offers of affection from comely women.

"Will you hang him now or wait 'til you've got Jordan and do them both together?" asked Mrs. Henderson with an eagerness that unsettled Cartwright.

"Our orders are to bring Kelly to Halifax to stand trial. Jordan has already been captured, it seems."

Mrs. Henderson was rather disappointed with the former piece of news, but thrilled with the latter. She seized Cartwright's hand and squeezed it.

"You do my heart good, sir. Every day George has been to sea since we heard of the *Three Sisters* business, I've prayed to God that he wouldn't run into that monster. Hanging's too good for him, I can tell you that! Tell me, sir—what does he look like, that terrible Ned Jordan?"

"I cannot tell you, for I have never laid eyes on the man."

"Do you suppose he looks like Blackbeard?"

Cartwright grew impatient with the conversation, realizing that Mrs. Henderson was not going to make good on her earlier offer of a kiss.

"Ma'am, we must not tarry. This man must be brought to justice as swiftly as possible."

"Oh yes! Of course, sir! I shall not keep you. God bless you, and safe journey to Halifax!"

The lieutenant tipped his hat again and the procession moved on.

What ill luck, thought Mrs. Henderson as she waved them off, that the menfolk were out fishing and missed all the excitement of the capture! At least she would have something to tell George that night when the boats came in.

She watched as Kelly was loaded into a boat and rowed out to the waiting schooner. The wind howled in the trees behind her house, blowing the shirts and tea towels full like sails. Again, she wished Cartwright and his men a speedy voyage to Halifax. Pirates must never be allowed to prosper or what would the world be coming to?

Chapter 13

November 10, 1809, Halifax—

A wintry chill had descended on Halifax when *Cuttle* returned to the great harbour bearing its sad burden of prisoners. Newspapers had made the citizens of Halifax aware of Jordan's capture and its particulars shortly after it took place, and his arrival aboard *Cuttle* was expected daily. Passing by Maugher's Beach as they entered the harbour, Jordan grimly noted that four fresh corpses had appeared on the beach gallows since he had come back from Gaspé in July. He stared at the swinging bodies with a strange sense of having lived the scene before. Why were these men familiar? They had certainly not been there when he and *Three Sisters* had sailed in triumph into Halifax Harbour. Then the air had been warm, and his mind had been filled with hope for the future. Today, with snow in the air and death so close he could almost taste it, Jordan felt a chill settling on his soul.

Margaret and Ned Jordan were incarcerated together in the drafty jail on the grounds of the poorhouse, while their four children were sent to the Catholic orphanage, their parents' fates still to be decided.

IN THE SITTING ROOM of his fine house on Barrington Street, Chief Justice Sampson Salter Blowers read of the news of Jordan's capture in the *Royal Gazette* as he took his morning tea. Though the weather had turned colder in recent days, Blowers did not ask the maid to light a fire in the massive fireplace near his chair to warm him. He would be going out in a few moments in any case, to meet with members of His Majesty's Council at Government House, and there was no sense in wasting the wood.

Finishing his tea and biscuit, Blowers folded the *Gazette* carefully and left it on the table along with the morning mail, still unopened. He stepped out into a cold late fall day, hatless and without an overcoat—he never wore one, even in the coldest weather. As he walked the short distance to Government House, Prevost's residence, the sixty-seven-year-old magistrate reflected on the Jordan case. Blowers had presided over many cases in his career as judge and had participated in many more as a skillful and respected trial lawyer. The majority of the cases brought before him were for debt—an unsurprising fact in these economically precarious days. The remainder usually involved trespassing, and occasionally, smuggling. The Jordan case, though, was entirely different. Piracy and murder were unusual crimes in Nova Scotia, and a special court would have to be convened to address them. Blowers was meeting with Governor Prevost and the council this morning to go over the particulars of the commission that would deal with Jordan. Uniacke would be there too, Blowers reflected, and a scowl passed over his face. The Attorney General of the province, Richard John Uniacke, was an old rival; when Blowers had himself been named to that position some years earlier instead of Uniacke, arousing his jealousy, the younger man had had harsh words for Blowers, and a bitter enmity had developed between the two men, so much so that they had come close to fighting each other in duels on two separate occasions. Blowers would have given much to be able to avoid the Attorney General, but their professions brought them into frequent and often uncomfortable contact.

As Blowers turned in the drive at Government House, he spotted Uniacke's tall figure striding purposefully toward the building from the opposite direction, and hastened to reach the door quickly so as not to encounter him. The doorman showed him into one of the first-floor chambers, where Prevost, Admiral Warren and several members of His Majesty's Council were already seated.

"Ah, Mr. Blowers, you have arrived. Splendid, splendid!" said Prevost, standing up to shake the chief justice's hand. "And Mr. Uniacke," he continued as the attorney-general was shown in by the doorman a few moments later, "you, too, are most welcome. Shall we begin, gentlemen?"

Blowers and Uniacke took their seats at opposite ends of the long mahogany table around which sat an august assembly of barristers, judges, and several captains of British frigates stationed in Halifax. They talked quietly amongst themselves, discreetly avoiding the subject of the well-known feud between Uniacke and Blowers.

Introductions were made by the governor for the benefit of the visiting British captains. Then Prevost got down to business.

"Gentlemen—we are met today to initiate proceedings in the court of vice-admiralty against Edward Jordan, the Irishman lately captured in Newfoundland on suspicion of piracy aboard the schooner *Three Sisters*, registered under the names of Jonathan and John Tremaine, merchants of this city."

Smirks appeared on the faces of two of the British post-captains at the mention of Jordan's nationality; indeed, they felt that most of their own impressed Irish sailors could turn mutinous if given the slightest chance. Uniacke, himself an Irish immigrant, caught the knowing looks passed among the captains and felt a surge of resentment.

Prevost continued. "It is also for us to determine the culpability of Jordan's wife, who, according to Captain Stairs, attacked and attempted to kill him with a boat hook."

A look of incredulity passed over the faces of the captains. To be attacked by a woman aboard one's own ship was strange enough as to be almost beyond the realm of possibility.

Briggs, the aged and rather slow-witted captain of HMS *Eolus*, now spoke. "Sirs, if I may inquire as to the precise circumstances of this unfortunate event: I have been at sea for weeks and heard nothing of the affair until this morning. Am I to understand that the wife of this Edward Jordan was aboard ship at the time of the mutiny?"

"*Alleged* mutiny," interjected Uniacke with a slight tone of exaggeration.

Briggs looked at Uniacke with bemusement, unused to being corrected.

"As you say, sir," he replied dismissively. Turning to Prevost, he asked, "What was this woman doing aboard ship?"

"She and the four Jordan children were travelling as passengers from Quebec to Halifax; the Tremaines had dealings with Jordan this summer and had engaged John Stairs of this city to bring back *Three Sisters* with a load of cod for their store. It seems that the brothers Tremaine did not place their full trust in Jordan—according to the testimony Stairs gave to the British consul in Boston, they engaged him partly to keep an eye on the Irishman so that no mischief should befall the ship whose title they hold."

Captain Briggs shook his head with reproach. "Bloody bad business, having a woman aboard. Can only stir up trouble."

Uniacke spoke again. "Sir, as you well know, many a passenger of the fair sex has safely crossed the Atlantic these many years in the company of men, and we in the New World must rejoice that they did so, for how else would our race have been perpetuated?"

He smiled innocuously at Briggs, who scowled back, saying nothing.

Prevost intervened. "Gentlemen—let us return to the matter at hand. Jordan, the mate Kelly, and Margaret Jordan have all been returned to Halifax and are awaiting trial. Because of the magnitude of the crimes they are supposed to have committed—the murder of two men, the attempted murder of a captain—I am sure you share my desire to see them expeditiously dealt with. I have brought you here today to solicit your assistance in trying the prisoners. We will begin hearing the case in no more than five days, as soon as the evidence can be assembled and Captain Stairs has had time to prepare himself. Of course, his testimony is of the utmost importance to the court; were it not for his miraculous rescue, we might never have known of the horrible deeds committed on this ship."

There was a pause as the assembly considered in sympathetic silence the ordeal undergone by Captain Stairs, a young man several of them knew personally.

The oblivious Captain Briggs now broke the silence, gesticulating in the air with one flabby arm.

"Yes! It comes to me now—Stairs is the man who jumped overboard to save himself from the miserable Irishman and his harridan wife; he was picked up by the Yankees floating on a booby-hatch. A damned lucky thing—and may I say that I would have Jordan and Kelly hanged from the yardarm as soon as I got my hands on them, before I wasted a moment of His Majesty's Council's time with a trial. Why, in fact, has it not already been done, sirs?"

Prevost looked uncomfortable, but Uniacke was quick with a reply.

"Captain, Jordan and Kelly were not members of His Majesty's navy; *Three Sisters* is a merchant ship, not a frigate. The alleged crimes were committed on the high seas; in such cases, protocol demands that a court of vice-admiralty be convened. This is our collective task: to see that Jordan, Kelly, and Margaret Jordan are tried in a court of law and are not the victims of rough justice."

"Little difference whether they were on a merchantman or a man-o'-war," Briggs persisted. "It's the same vermin crawling on both, and both deserve the same treatment, in my book: hanging."

Uniacke flushed. "It is all very well for a captain of the navy to speak thus, but as a lawyer representing the people of Nova Scotia, I am necessarily of a different mind than you, sir."

Briggs crossed his arms belligerently, and with a scoffing expression, jeered.

"Lawyers, lawyers—I've had my fill of lawyers. Out to line their pockets with the hard-earned money of the working man. Most of 'em are no better than criminals."

Uniacke looked genuinely outraged and was about to reply with his views on the barbarity of the Royal Navy when he was interrupted by his old foe Blowers, who rose up from the table suddenly.

"Mr. Uniacke, Captain Briggs: I respectfully ask you to reserve your grievances until such time as you may find a more private forum in which to air them. We have more pressing matters to attend to presently."

Uniacke and Briggs simmered angrily, but were silent.

Blowers took his seat, and smiled condescendingly at Uniacke. The Attorney General could not bring himself to look at Blowers. How he hated his smugness!

Prevost looked gratefully at Blowers, noting again the graceful diplomacy and ease of expression for which the chief justice was known.

"Thank you, Mr. Blowers. Now, may I know how many of you gentlemen will be in attendance at next week's hearing by a show of hands?"

The hands of all fifteen men were raised. Prevost looked gratified.

"Thank you, gentlemen. Now that this unpleasant business is completed, shall we adjourn to the drawing room and take a glass of sherry?"

Blowers rose again, this time with his regrets. "Thank you, Governor—but I regret that I must take my leave of you presently. I am called to make a preliminary examination of the prisoners this afternoon and must prepare myself for the task."

Prevost rose to shake the hand of the chief justice, who bowed to the assembled dignitaries before taking his leave.

THE PRISON WHERE the Jordans and Kelly were incarcerated was a cold and drafty edifice, better suited as a warehouse than as housing for human beings. Margaret Jordan paced about her cell like a caged lioness, frantic to be separated from her children. She was one of the only female inmates then housed at the prison and received lascivious looks from the male prisoners, some of whom had not been in such close quarters with a woman for many months.

She seemed barely aware of her surroundings, adrift in an unhappy world of her own.

Kelly lay on his cot for days, refusing to eat and take exercise, staring continually at the high ceiling of the narrow cell he shared with Jordan, who was quite certain that his cellmate would again attempt to take his own life. He warned the warden of Kelly's suicidal tendencies so that no knife ever passed into the cell along with the prisoners' meagre meals.

On the third morning of her imprisonment, Margaret Jordan woke from a fitful sleep to the sound of carriage wheels and horses' hooves clattering over stone. Peering from the narrow slit in the stone wall separating her from the world, she saw a well-dressed gentleman alight from the carriage and enter the prison, accompanied by the warden, who had come out to greet him.

A few minutes later, she heard the warden's key turning in the lock of her cell door, which swung open to reveal a grave-looking official wearing a heavy grey overcoat and carrying a notebook in his gloved hand. His speech was witheringly formal.

"Margaret Jordan—it is my duty to bring you, your husband, and John Kelly before Mr. Justice Blowers to be examined before your trial on charges of piracy commences. You will accompany me to the council chamber immediately."

"And who are you, sir?" asked Margaret in a wary voice.

"I am a magistrate for the town of Halifax. My name is Jones."

"Very well, Mr. Jones. I see that I have not much choice in the matter."

Margaret picked up a thin shawl from the bottom of her cot and draped it across her narrow shoulders before accompanying Jones and the warden to the yard, where a closed, windowless wagon waited for her. She noted ruefully that she would not be travelling in the magistrate's well-appointed carriage.

After Ned Jordan and John Kelly had joined her in the wagon, their hands bound, their faces sombre, the two horse-drawn vehicles began their short journey to the offices of the chief justice.

Margaret, who had not said more than two words to her husband since their capture, now spoke to him anxiously, in a low voice. "Ah, Ned—what shall I say to the judge?"

"Say whatever you please; it makes no difference now," replied her husband flatly, not looking at her.

"Maybe for you, it doesn't—but I still have the children to think about. I'll say whatever I must to save myself from the gallows and them from the orphanage."

"They're already at the orphanage, Margaret," said Jordan. "Have you so soon forgotten? They'll be wards of the state now—and it may well be a better life for them."

Margaret burst into tears. "How can you speak so heartlessly of your own flesh and blood, you murdering bastard?"

Jordan looked at his wife with resignation. "I have not the strength to fight you now, Margaret. You know well I did what I could for those children, my Maggie especially. It breaks my heart that I am to be forever separated from them. Can you not allow me even a moment's peace?"

Margaret lapsed into tearful silence, her rough hands twisting and untwisting her ragged shawl.

Once arrived at the offices, the prisoners were brought into a small room to await the will of Chief Justice Blowers. As they entered, Margaret was stunned with joy to find Neddy already waiting and enveloped him in her thin arms with joy and gratitude. Clasping him tightly to her breast, Margaret asked the boy, "Where are your sisters, Neddy?"

Neddy looked sad. "At th'orphanage."

"Why, boy, are you here and not they?" said his mother, baffled.

The boy bowed his head and was silent.

Jones now spoke. "The boy is to be examined by Justice Blowers, as he witnessed the murders of Heath and Matthews, and is at the age of understanding. His sisters are too young to comprehend the magnitude of their father's crimes."

Margaret turned on Jones with anger. "You'll not bring my child into a courtroom! It ain't right, sir! No, it ain't right to turn a child against his parents."

Jones looked dispassionately at the distraught woman before him. "I'm afraid you have no say in the matter, ma'am. Justice Blowers asked for the lad to be brought here to examine him, and it has been done. It is up to him to decide how to proceed."

As the magistrate finished speaking, a heavy oak door swung open, and the voice of Chief Justice Sampson Blowers was heard calling from within the dark, wood-panelled inner chamber,

"Bring the woman in first, Jones, if you please."

Margaret shook as she was brought before the judge, both from anger on her son's behalf and fear for their fate.

She spoke shakily, unable to contain herself, "It ain't right, judge, you bringing my son Neddy here to try to get him to speak lies against his mother and father."

Blowers, seated behind his desk, and nearly hidden behind several sizeable mounds of books and briefs, now removed his spectacles and looked inquisitively at Margaret.

"Isn't it, Mrs. Jordan? Your son was one of the few witnesses to a pair of horrible murders. Besides yourself, he and Captain Stairs are the only two people, besides your daughters, who are not of age, who were present at the time of the killings and the attempted killing of Mr. Stairs. Can you not see how his testimony is of the utmost importance to the prosecution?"

"He's only nine!" protested Margaret. "He's still a child, Judge."

"The Church tells us that a person reaches the age of understanding by age seven," countered Blowers. "Your son is well above that age, Mrs. Jordan."

"I don't care what you say, Judge. Neddy will never turn against his father and mother."

"Mrs. Jordan, you may be sure that I and Mr. Stewart will treat your son with care and sympathy to the difficult circumstance in which he has been placed."

"Who's this Mr. Stewart, Judge?"

"He is the Solicitor General for the province, and will be conducting the prosecution's case."

"And we—my husband and I—have we a lawyer too?"

"Yes, ma'am—Mr. Wilkins has been appointed as your counsel, and Mr. Robie will serve as your husband's defender."

"What about Kelly?"

"He is to be tried separately and at a later date. He has not yet been appointed counsel."

Margaret sat back in her chair, absorbing this information.

Pulling a thick sheaf of papers from a pile on his desk, Blowers cleared his throat and began.

"Now, Mrs. Jordan—to return to the events of the thirteenth of September just past. John Stairs alleges that you attempted to kill crewman Matthews with a pistol, then attacked him with a boathook as he and your husband were engaged in a struggle for mastery of the ship."

"The bastard stabbed me in the leg! I was forced to defend myself," Margaret replied hoarsely. "I can show you where he done it." Jumping up from her chair, she hoisted up her skirts and pointed to an angry, red wound still in the process of healing on her mid-thigh. Blowers looked profoundly embarrassed at this show of indecency and tried to avert his eyes.

"There is no need to uncover yourself in such a way, Mrs. Jordan," he said in a low voice.

"Why not?" shrugged Margaret, lowering her skirts again. "You'll see me hanged ere long, Judge, and my whitening bones pecked over by the crows and gulls." She laughed bitterly. "That'll be quite an uncovering, now won't it, sir?"

"No one is accusing you of murder, Mrs. Jordan," protested the chief justice. "It is your husband we are interested in on that score. No, I am merely here to examine you with respect to Captain Stairs' allegations that you attacked him with a deadly weapon in your hand."

"That I did, that I did, good sir," sighed Margaret, sinking back into her seat limply.

"And why, ma'am, did you do so?"

"Why, it was purely self-defence, Judge," said Margaret, her eyes wide and expectant.

"Did Captain Stairs ever lay a hand on you while you and he were aboard *Three Sisters?*"

"Not in the way that you suggest, sir. His intentions were more passionate than violent, I would say."

Blowers looked shocked. From another pile on his desk, he pulled out a sheaf of notes taken earlier in the week during an interview with John Stairs, recounting the events of September 13. He rifled through them intently.

"Mrs. Jordan—it would seem that you and Captain Stairs are in disagreement on this point. When Mr. Stewart and I spoke with him two days ago, he told us that it was you who consistently made advances upon him, angering your husband. He says that he always rebuffed these advances, that he would have nothing to do with a married woman, nor one who..."

Blowers checked himself before reading back to Margaret the passage in his notes where the angered Stairs spoke of his revulsion at the mere thought of sharing his bed with a dirty Irishwoman.

Margaret's face flushed with anger and humiliation.

"He's a liar, Judge, if he denies wanting me. It was I who had to push him away, to warn him of my husband's anger if we was ever discovered. You ask Neddy—he'll tell you he saw Stairs taking liberties with me in the cabin the very morning of the killings. He went right to his father with it, and that's what set him off on his rampage."

Blowers stared at Margaret with disbelief plainly written on his face. He was certain that she was lying to him; Stairs had left him in no doubt as to the true version of events. Though, as far as testimony went, it was Stairs' word against Margaret's, the chief justice was certainly more willing to believe the word of the son of a good Halifax family than that of a poverty-stricken Irishwoman.

He jotted down a few remarks in his notebook, then rose from his chair.

"Mrs. Jordan—these are very serious allegations you make against Captain Stairs; however, I am obliged to take them under advisement. I will be sure to pass along your story to your counsel, Mr. Wilkins and to Mr. Robie."

"How soon before I can see my daughters, sir?" asked Margaret, ignoring his words, and with a pleading look in her eyes.

"I cannot answer," said Blowers.

"I hope I live to see the day Ned Jordan is hanged," said Margaret quietly, as though she were speaking to herself.

Rising from her chair, she slowly approached the chief justice, rolling up the sleeves of her dirty calico dress as she did so.

Blowers was horrified to see the geography of bruises, cuts and abrasions she revealed—wounds he recognized clearly as those associated with domestic violence.

Seized by a kind of desperate sadness that threatened to suffocate him, he made a quick movement toward the door, eager to be rid of his pathetic prisoner.

"Thank you, Mrs. Jordan," he said. "You may return to your seat with the other prisoners. I will speak with your son Edward now."

He gestured to the unhappy boy who sat slumped on a bench in the corner of the anteroom. With a nervous and unwilling expression, Neddy followed the judge into the dark chamber, the heavy door clicking shut behind him.

Chapter 14

November 15, 1809, Halifax—

Early on a Wednesday morning, the first day of the trial for piracy of Edward and Margaret Jordan, Captain Briggs donned his best blue dress uniform and gave his wig an extra dusting before setting it firmly atop his glistening bald head. From his well-appointed quarters near the naval yard, it was only a short carriage ride to the makeshift courthouse on Hollis Street where the pair of prisoners would be tried. The mud on the well-rutted road had now frozen over, making for a bumpy ride punctuated by sudden jolts as the wooden wheels crested the mountain range of hard, churned up earth and then fell sharply over the other side. Briggs dozed fitfully inside the carriage, still recovering from the effects of dinner at the admiral's house the evening before.

The horses came to a stop in front of the Cochrane Building, where several other carriages were already in the process of drawing up and an assortment of naval officers were alighting from them. All of them, like Captain Briggs, were attired in their best full-dress uniform. The admiral of the station, Sir John Borlase Warren, had arrived early in the company of two officers, and together they had made a fulsome entrance into the court building.

By the time of Briggs' arrival, a crowd of townspeople had gathered across the street to watch the dignitaries assembling, and in the hopes of catching a glimpse of the two prisoners most of them had only heard about in the papers. The Jordans' former landlady, Mrs. Zinck, was one of these spectators, and having known the couple personally, as many of those gathered about her had not, she did not share in their prevailing sentiments.

"Good riddance to bad rubbish is what I say about that dreadful Jordan pair," said one righteous soul perched on the stone ledge of a building adjoining the court. "The day they hang 'em will be a good one for this city and for the world."

Mrs. Zinck turned to the speaker, her face scarlet with anger.

"I beg your pardon, ma'am, but I never knew a more hardworking woman than Margaret Jordan, nor a more loving mother. Sure, Jordan was a ne'er-do-well, but it was she and the children who had to bear that burden—and it was only when his little girl was so badly burned that he grew mad in his grief."

The woman sitting on the window ledge stared at Mrs. Zinck as though she had grown another head.

"And, begging your pardon, ma'am—how would you be knowing so much about the Jordan family?"

"They let rooms from me this year, before this terrible business on the ship. I helped nurse the little girl when she was burned. A sweet child—my heart aches for her and her sisters and brother and what they will have to endure when their parents are gone."

Disconcerted, the woman on the ledge said nothing. She had not thought of what would happen to the children when their parents were hanged.

As it happened, the spectators on Hollis Street would be denied their look at the prisoners that morning; Ned and Margaret Jordan were brought into the courthouse through a side door well removed from the public's curious gaze. Neither of the Jordans had slept the previous night and both had the pallor of heavy anxiety painted on their faces. Their shabby homespun clothes contrasted strongly with the sartorial splendour of those who would sit in judgement on them—that same assembly of Halifax lawyers and English captains who had met at Government House five days earlier.

When they were brought into the courtroom in the company of their lawyers, a second group of spectators was waiting in the gallery, eager for a look at the notorious pirates who had killed two men in cold blood and had nearly succeeded in killing their well-respected fellow townsman, John Stairs. Many in the crowd were especially anxious to see Margaret Jordan, whose sex made her alleged crimes still more vile, in their eyes. They finally got their look at the woman as she was led into the prisoners' box, manacled, her thin shoulders stooped, and looking extremely vulnerable. Many of the spectators did not believe that such a frail creature could have attacked a sea captain; indeed, she looked barely robust enough to swat a fly.

Ned Jordan's appearance in the courtroom stirred up a gust of ire among the spectators, and a hiss of opprobrium seemed to collectively pass their lips as he was led past them.

The entrance into the courtroom of the fifteen-man committee that would serve as judge and jury was heralded by the sound of clanking medals and the clicking of well-heeled boots on the wooden floors. Admiral Warren led the group, followed by Governor Prevost, Chief Justice Blowers, Attorney General Uniacke, and the remaining eleven dignitaries. Once the members of the commission had taken their seats, the president of the commission, Governor Prevost, rose to speak.

"By the grace of God, in this the year of Our Lord eighteen hundred and nine, and under the Acts of our former most gracious sovereigns William and Mary, we have gathered this day to convene a special court of vice-admiralty for the trial of Edward Jordan and his wife, Margaret. I will present to the court the charges laid against Edward and Margaret Jordan: they are hereby formally accused of piracy and murder for their actions at sea aboard the schooner *Three Sisters*, on September the 13th of the present year. Edward Jordan is accused of firing upon and killing seamen Thomas Heath and Benjamin Matthews and attempting to kill Captain John Stairs, who in self-defence was obliged to jump overboard. Margaret Jordan is charged with aiding and abetting her husband in his attempt on Captain Stairs' life by striking at him with a boat hook."

Here a murmur of shocked disbelief rose from the gallery.

Pausing a moment for effect, Prevost continued. "It is the purpose of today's proceedings to arraign Edward and Margaret Jordan on the aforementioned charges and to determine which way they plead, guilty or not guilty. Mr. Wilkins, Mr. Robie," Prevost addressed the two defense lawyers who sat near their clients, "how do the prisoners plead?"

Robie stood first and said, "My charge, Edward Jordan, pleads not guilty, your honours."

Wilkins' response was the same: "Margaret Jordan also pleads not guilty, your honours."

"Be it recorded that the prisoners have entered pleas of not guilty," said Prevost, gesturing to the court scribe, who was writing feverishly in his ledger.

The Solicitor General for the province, James Stewart, next read out the names of witnesses to be examined at the court's next meeting: they included John Pigot and Patrick Power, the seamen Jordan had engaged in Newfoundland, and, of course, John Stairs on whose testimony the prosecution's case hung. These formalities being accomplished, the court was adjourned until the next day.

The committee clanked out of the courtroom and the prisoners were led away, their faces still ashen.

WHEN THE COURT RECONVENED the following day, all were anxious to hear the testimony of John Stairs, the man who had nearly become Ned Jordan's third victim. On the witness stand, Stairs appeared calm, though his pallor suggested the many sleepless nights he had undergone since his ordeal.

Solicitor general Stewart began his questioning.

"What is your profession and occupation in life?"

"A mariner and ship master," replied Stairs.

"What ship did you last command?"

"The schooner *Three Sisters.*"

"Who gave you the command of the *Three Sisters?*"

"Jonathan and John Tremaine."

"On what voyage did you sail with her?"

"To Perce, for the purpose of procuring a cargo of fish Jordan had promised to deliver. We sailed on the seventeenth of July."

"Who sailed with you on the schooner?"

"John Kelly, mate, Thomas Heath, seaman, and pilot, Benjamin Matthews, seaman, and Edward Jordan and his family, as passengers."

"Did you take in a cargo at Perce?"

"Part of a cargo, yes—five hundred quintals of fish on the account of the owners of the ship, J. and J. Tremaine."

Jordan felt a pang of sadness at Stairs' words; even now, it was hard to accept that his beloved *Three Sisters* belonged not to him but to his creditors.

The questioning of the witness continued.

"When did you sail from Perce?"

"On the tenth of September, for Halifax."

Stewart paused for a moment, looking intently at Stairs when he spoke.

"Relate, fully and distinctly, all the circumstances that occurred on your voyage from Perce to Halifax."

Stairs cleared his throat and began to recount the tale of his journey aboard *Three Sisters* and of Jordan's treachery. His clear voice could be heard distinctly even by those seated at the rear of the gallery. A murmur of horror passed through the courtroom when Stairs spoke of the death of the first seaman and repeated Heath's final words, "Oh God, I am killed!"

Stairs went on to describe his shock on discovering that his pistols had been stolen from the cabin. His jaw clenched, feeling again a measure of his first anger at discovering Jordan's treachery. He refused to look at the accused man now. In relating the story of Kelly's refusal to come to his aid, the death of Matthews and Margaret's attack on him with a boat hook—events now indelibly etched in his mind—Stairs felt as though he were reliving them, moment by moment.

The gallery recommenced its horrified whispering at this confirmation of Jordan's wife's inhumanity. Margaret felt the hot stares of their reproach scalding her face and neck.

Stairs continued his testimony—how he had jumped overboard and floated for he knew not how long until he was rescued by the American schooner *Eliza*, an act of mercy for which he thanked the Almighty. With some hesitation, he described Captain Stoddard's reluctance to pursue the fleeing *Three Sisters* because of the danger to his ship and crew. Stairs then described the foul weather that had persisted in the days following his rescue, how Stoddard had been unable to land him in Nova Scotia, how he had arrived in Boston and told his story to the British consul there. His story at an end, Stairs sat back in his chair.

Silence now prevailed in the courtroom, those present scarcely able to believe what the young man seated before them had had to endure at the hands of the prisoner. That he had survived to tell the tale at all was certainly miraculous.

Solicitor general Stewart, who had been listening with the same rapt attention as everyone present, now spoke. "Returning to your earlier testimony, if you please, Captain Stairs. Had there, previous to the firing of the pistol, been any dispute or quarrel between you and the prisoner, Edward Jordan?"

Stairs looked at Stewart; then he turned and looked at Jordan for the first time that morning. He replied, "There had not."

Jordan shook his head with contempt, muttering in a nearly inaudible voice, "Lies, lies…" The Solicitor General turned to Jordan and asked, "Is there something you would like to say, Mr. Jordan?"

"No, sir."

"In that case, the prisoner will keep silent until such time as he is asked to give his own testimony to the court."

Turning back to Stairs, Stewart asked, "Captain Stairs, what exchanges, if any, did you have with Margaret Jordan prior to September the 13ᵗʰ?"

Stairs looked uncomfortable.

"We spoke only in passing as I was occupied with the smooth running of the ship."

"Can you give any indication of why she might have struck you several blows with a boat hook?"

Stairs looked at the gaunt figure of Margaret Jordan in the prisoners' box and felt within him combined weariness and pity, emotions that took him greatly by surprise. During the three agonizing hours of his ordeal at sea, as he clung shivering to the floating hatch, his hatred for the Jordans and desire to see them both hanged had kept his body warm. Now, two months later, Stairs wanted only to have done with the terrible affair, and while he could not forgive Jordan, he felt somewhat more lenient toward his wife.

"Mr. Stewart—I cannot tell what Mrs. Jordan must have been thinking on that day. I suspect she may have lost her mind in the heat of the moment."

"Were you injured by the blows you received from her?"

"No. She is not a strong woman."

He looked across at Margaret again. She had tears in her eyes.

After Jordan's counsel, S. B. Robie briefly questioned Stairs; in his turn, the president of the commission, Governor Prevost, thanked the captain for his testimony and dismissed him. Stairs bowed to the court and was shown out of the courtroom by the marshal. He had no desire to be in Jordan's presence any longer than was necessary.

The next witness to be called was John Pigot, who twitched nervously as he took his oath.

Stewart began the interrogation.

"What is your occupation?"

"A fisherman and labourer at Bay of Bulls, Newfoundland."

"How long since you left your home?"

"Eight weeks tomorrow."

"In whose company did you leave it?"

"In the prisoner's."

"Relate to the court how you became acquainted with the prisoners, and what dealings you have had with them."

Pigot shifted uneasily in his chair. He felt Jordan's black eyes upon him and he stammered slightly as he spoke.

"I met the prisoner Edward Tremaine—I mean, Edward Jordan—around the end of September last, in Bay of Bulls, at old Hodges' tavern. At first he told me he was the owner of a fishing schooner and that he was short of hands. So we agreed I would ship with him on *Three Sisters* and procure my passage to Halifax, which he told me was our destination. Later, he changed his mind about where we was going, which he did often—first it was Halifax, then St John's, then Ireland. I didn't like it, and neither did the other men, Crew and Power. When I saw how carelessly the fish was stowed in the hold on my first day on the schooner, and then shortly afterwards found a rifle concealed among the fish, I could not help but become suspicious. I told Tremaine, I mean Jordan, that I suspected the schooner was on the runaway account and that I wished no further dealings with him. He threatened me and told me he'd see me impressed on the next man-of-war to make port in Bay of Bulls, or words to that effect. I repeated that I did not wish to serve on a ship that was running from the law. Jordan threatened me again, and having no recourse, I was obliged to stay."

Pigot looked at the ground, unwilling to meet the eyes of Jordan, who sat only a few feet away.

Stewart continued. "Mr. Pigot, what exchanges, if any, did you have with the prisoner Margaret Jordan while on board *Three Sisters*?"

"Several, sir. I can tell the court that it was my impression—and Crew and Power will say the same, I'm sure—that she was very ill-used by Jordan. We observed that she had a number of bad cuts and bruises on her arms and face, and Power heard some terrible arguments between the two of them before I arrived."

"Mr. Pigot, I asked if you had any direct exchanges with Margaret Jordan while you were serving on board *Three Sisters*. You have spoken so far only of your observations of the prisoner."

"Well yes, sir—we did converse several times after we left Bay of Bulls and before we were captured. She told me once that I had no idea the kind of life she led with that man—her husband—and that she was the only person who could hang him. For that, she said he threatened to kill her."

Pigot looked over at Margaret Jordan, who had begun wringing her hands as though she were squeezing water out of wet sheets. She looked imploringly back at him, her desperation palpable. He shifted uncomfortably in his seat.

"Did she explain what was intended by the statement that she was the only person who could hang him?"

"No, sir—I did ask what she meant by it after she said it to me, but she clammed up and wouldn't say any more. It rather chilled me, though, to hear her say it. I thought then Jordan must have killed a man and was hiding his crime from the world, or at least, was trying to."

Stewart continued. "During the time of your sailing aboard *Three Sisters*, did you ever observe Edward Jordan drunk?"

"Every day, sir."

"Did Margaret Jordan ever speak to you of the murders aboard *Three Sisters* which took place on September the 13th?"

"No, sir."

"Did she ever speak to you of her attack on Captain Stairs on that day, September 13th?"

"No, sir."

"Thank you, Mr. Pigot. The Crown rests."

When Patrick Power was summoned to give testimony against Edward Jordan, his story was much the same as Pigot's had been: taken together, the seamen's accounts painted a consistent portrait of a disturbed and desperate man who regularly beat his wife and gave every indication of the kind of murderous personality he had displayed on September 13.

When Power had taken his seat, Edward Jordan was summoned

to the bar. Every ear in the courtroom now strained to hear the account of the prisoner's heinous crimes from his own lips.

The solicitor general addressed Jordan immediately after he had been sworn in.

"State your name, for the record, please."

"Edward Jordan."

"Have you ever used an alias?"

"Edward Tremaine."

"Mr. Jordan, you are being tried for the murders of Thomas Heath and Benjamin Matthews and for the attempted murder of John Stairs on September the 13th of the present year. We heard Captain Stairs' testimony yesterday, relating the events of that day as he experienced them. Is there anything you would like to add to his account of events?"

"Yes, sir—there is." Jordan retrieved from his pocket a dirty piece of paper upon which he had carefully written down the story he would tell to the court. He was about to take a desperate gamble.

"I would like to say that John Stairs did himself and this court a disservice when he stated that he and I had had no quarrel prior to September the 13th. It was many days prior to September the 13th that he surreptitiously obtained the deed to my ship, *Three Sisters*, for the benefit of his employers, Jonathan and John Tremaine, and deprived me of my rightful property and means of employment. This situation brought me to the edge of despair and I began drinking. On the morning in question, being rather in liquor, I was sitting on the quarterdeck when my little boy came running to tell me that he had just seen Captain Stairs taking liberties with his mother. Seized with an anger I might not have felt so strongly had I been sober, I swiftly made my way to the cabin, where I found Stairs forcing himself upon my wife, who was screaming, whereupon I seized him and threw him to the floor. When he had recovered, the captain rushed to his trunk for his pistol, which he fired at me. His aim was off—he missed me, but struck Thomas Heath in the breast, killing him."

"Do you deny killing Thomas Heath yourself, Mr. Jordan?"

"It was Stairs that killed him, Mr. Stewart, by accident—as I said, he was aiming for me."

"What was Heath doing in the cabin, Mr. Jordan?"

"Hearing my wife's cries, he had rushed to her assistance but a few moments earlier. For this, he received death."

"Continue, Mr. Jordan."

"Stairs chased me up the companionway to the deck, where I had gone to find a handspike to defend myself with, but Stairs caught up with me and we struggled for possession of the pistol. In the struggle, the gun went off and struck poor Ben Matthews in the head. When I finally succeeded in wresting the weapon from the captain, he very unexpectedly grabbed a hatch and threw it into the water, then jumped in after it. I begged Kelly, who was at the wheel, to put the vessel about and pick up the captain."

"What did Kelly say to this?"

"He said he would not do as I asked—that we would all be lost by this course of action, and the ship continued on its course."

"When did you and John Kelly part company?"

"Some days later, when we made land at Bay of Bulls."

"What did you say to Kelly, and he to you, at the time of your parting?"

"There was no parting—he ran off the same day we arrived. He was not in his right mind."

"Not in his right mind since the time of the killings, would you say?"

"Perhaps even before then, I would say."

"Mr. Jordan, you have heard the testimony of John Pigot and Patrick Power relating to your dealings with them while you were in port at Bay of Bulls. Can you offer any clarification of Mr. Pigot's statement that your wife told him she feared for her life at your hands, or for her statement that she was the only person who could see you hang?"

"No reliance can be placed on the evidence of those witnesses—Pigot and Power—just as no reliance can be placed on the word of

John Kelly, who is mad. They have made up their story; they would say anything that came into their heads."

"And why would they do that, Mr. Jordan?"

Jordan ignored the question. "Mr. Solicitor General, I have some papers here that I wish to submit to the court: they contain my accounts with the Tremaines, among other things. I wish that the honourable members of the court examine them before coming to a decision in my case. As for the rest, I have nothing further to say."

Jordan gestured to his counsel, who rose and handed a small sheaf of papers to Governor Prevost.

"Very well, Mr. Jordan. You are dismissed."

Margaret Jordan was the next to be questioned by the solicitor general.

"Mrs. Jordan, have you anything to say to the court in your own behalf in relation to your part in the events of September the 13th aboard *Three Sisters*?"

Margaret gestured to her counsel, Lewis Wilkins, who rose from his seat with a single sheet of paper in his hand. "If it please the court, Mrs. Jordan has given me a written statement which I will read on her behalf, she not being able to read nor write:

"'My name is Margaret Jordan. I married Edward Jordan ten years ago in Ireland and lived happily with him for five. Then we removed to the United States, where he soon became unhappy and jealous of me, and I have received severe treatment from him ever since.

"'On the morning of September the 13th, as I lay ill after he had struck me several blows the night before, Captain Stairs came to my berth. I was alarmed that his presence there would arouse my husband's jealousy, and begged him to be gone, and soon my husband appeared, enraged and instantly knocked Stairs down. He was followed a few minutes later by Thomas Heath, and after Stairs had grabbed a pistol from his trunk, he shot at my husband, but missed him and struck Heath in the chest, killing him. After that, I cannot fully tell what occurred. Stairs and my husband left the cabin running hard, and I heard another shot from above deck and ran up, fearing for the safety of my poor children. I cannot deny but that I might have struck Stairs when he was struggling with my husband, as I was then in such a state of mind as not to know what I was doing. I can, however, appeal to the Almighty and say that I am innocent of the crime of piracy of which I now stand charged.'"

There was silence in the room for a few moments after Wilkins finished reading Margaret Jordan's statement and had taken his seat once more. The story she had told her lawyer was the one she felt was the least damaging to herself and her role in the attack on Stairs, though she knew it differed significantly from the events of September 13 as they actually occurred. She clung to her defence of temporary insanity as to a thin lifeline that would save her from the gallows.

Prevost thanked both counsels and the witnesses for their services to the court, which he then dismissed; he and the other members of the commission recessed into a private chamber for their deliberation. The subdued spectators watched their exit, many filled with nervous anticipation, and some with outright awe at the power wielded by these men dressed in the sober robes of office lined with red and trimmed with ermine. They could not help but note the contrast between these men of influence and Edward and Margaret Jordan, whose fate now lay in their hands. No one moved from his seat.

"Gentlemen, the court is adjourned," said the marshal in a booming voice after the prisoners had been led from their box. "Kindly leave the premises while the committee deliberates."

Picking up their coats and hats and filing out of the courtroom, the men spoke quietly among themselves.

"I don't believe a word of Jordan's story, do you, Harry?" said one middle-aged man with ginger whiskers to his companion.

"Certainly not! A fine young man like John Stairs wanting anything to do with that trashy woman? Bah! It don't hold water."

"How long'll it take 'em to reach a decision, do you suppose?"

"Don't know—maybe hours. Jordan's guilty as sin, that much is evident. It may puzzle them what to do with his wife. It don't look like she had anything to do with the murders, and there's her four children to consider if both parents hang for this. The last thing Halifax needs is more Irish orphans to support."

His companion nodded. "It's a sad business, Abe, a sad business. Think I'll go home for tea; it'll be good to stretch my legs and they'll not have reached a decision before four o'clock, I'll wager. That gives me a good two hours."

The ginger-whiskered man looked doubtful. "I'm not so sure about that, Harry. Think I'll wait out front a bit—I have a feeling it won't take them long, and I want to be here for the verdict."

"Suit yourself," said his friend. "I'm off." He strode away, leaving his companion on the steps of the courthouse with a few other stalwarts, shivering, for he had come away from home that morning without his hat and gloves.

Slipping out of the gallery after most of the others had gone, a tall and lanky figure in a woollen cap now quietly exited the courthouse and walked briskly back to his place of business. It was John Tremaine, who had silently observed the court proceedings from the beginning. The trial troubled him greatly and he would speak of it to no one, not even his brother, who refused to attend. John Tremaine knew already what the outcome would be; he would not be present for the sentencing.

THE SHIVERING GINGER-WHISKERED man was only half an hour in the cold before the marshal opened the great oak doors and informed the men on the steps that the committee had reached a decision.

"Abe will be sorry!" he thought, ruefully. "He will have barely sat down for his tea."

The prisoners were brought in; the committee filed into the courtroom again, its mind made up. Prevost spoke for them all.

"Will the prisoners please stand?"

The couple rose slowly from their seats, as though unwilling to hear the verdict. A million whirling pictures spun through Jordan's head, scenes from his life—or lives—in Ireland, Quebec, New York, Halifax, Newfoundland. They had all passed by so quickly, these thirty-eight years of his life—he could hardly account for where they had gone. He felt that he had lived a very long time and seen much more than a man should have to see. So much had not been his fault, and yet, he knew everyone in the courtroom would blame him for all of it. He tried to concentrate as Prevost read the verdict from a sheet of paper held in his right hand.

"Edward Jordan—the gentlemen commissioners before whom you have been accused of piracy and murder have lately examined the articles of charge exhibited against you, and having weighed and considered the several evidences produced against you on behalf of His Majesty, as well as what has been alleged in your favour, have unanimously found you guilty of the several articles of piracy wherewith you are charged, and have agreed that sentence should be pronounced against you for the same accordingly. Nothing therefore now remains but for me, as President of this court, to perform the painful duty of pronouncing the dreadful sentence which the law directs to be executed upon you as a just punishment for the horrid crimes of which you have been this day convicted, but as an example to all others of the vengeance which always pursues the steps of the murderer, whom no art can save from the sword of justice in this life, and whose only hope in the world to come must depend on the mercies of the Almighty. You, who have shown neither mercy nor compassion to your fellow creatures, can have none to expect from the hand of man. Let me, therefore, exhort you, during the short time you have to live, that you do with a contrite and penitent heart humble yourself before God and seek forgiveness of your sins through the merits and intercession of our blessed Savior, Jesus Christ.

"You, Edward Jordan, shall be taken from hence to the place from whence you came, and from thence to the place of execution, there to be hanged by the neck until you are dead—and may God Almighty have mercy upon your soul."

At the word "hanged," Jordan felt a jolt of dizziness and sunk to his chair, stunned. It was the second time in his life that he had faced hanging, and this time, there was no escaping his fate. Standing next to him, Margaret began to weep.

Prevost continued to read.

"Margaret Jordan—the court has considered also the charges brought against you, that you aided and abetted your husband, Edward Jordan, in his despicable acts of piracy and murder on board *Three Sisters*. The court finds you not guilty of these charges, and releases you from prison forthwith."

Margaret gave a little cry as the words "not guilty" were read, and, with her manacled hands, reached for her counsel, Lewis Wilkins, as though to embrace him.

THE CONTRAST IN THE TWO VERDICTS—the great and awful judgement imposed by the former, and the promise of freedom contained in the latter—struck everyone in the spectators' gallery. It was a moment none of them could ever forget.

Epilogue

Thursday, November 23, 1809, Halifax—

The wind coming off the unsettled ocean howled through the shaken trees like the banshees Ned Jordan's mother had often told him stories about when he was a child. It drove the swift-moving waves onto the shore at Black Rock Beach where the gallows had been built, near the mouth of the great harbour where for sixty years British ships had anchored in safety, protected from the fierce North Atlantic storms.

From the platform where he stood, Jordan could see the four scarecrow bodies of his old nightmare dangling from the gibbet on the shores of McNab's Island. He felt the same chill in his bones as he had ten years ago, waking up from his terrible dream. For a moment, he believed that this was a dream, too—that in a few moments, he would wake up, safe in the straw of Byrne's barn or in Margaret's arms. How pleasant it would be to stay asleep, to sleep forever, untroubled by the cares of the world—the worries about money, the sorrows for his children. He felt the rope tighten around his neck as he listened to the words of the Lord's Prayer recited by the priest who had accompanied him to the base of the gallows but no further. His eyes were on the ocean, watching a graceful schooner, her sails full, breasting the waves like a great seabird, entirely in its element. Freedom! When in his life had he ever experienced it?

When the platform fell away at last, Jordan felt himself unfurl, like the sail of a ship. It was here; he was free.

The crowd around him, which he had not noticed, stood silently while the wind swung him gently like a pendulum.

They wrapped his body in chains to preserve it for as long a time as possible: like the four on Maugher's Beach, this shamed body strung up at the mouth of the harbour would be made to do its duty, warning all comers of the wages of piracy.

SEVERAL WEEKS AFTER THE HANGING, Margaret Jordan and her children sailed from Halifax to Ireland, their passage paid for by the charity of the citizens of Halifax, who hoped never to hear of the Jordan family again. One of the largest donations came from John Tremaine. As their crowded ship passed by Point Pleasant, where their father and husband hung in shame, the Jordan family huddled in the hold, avoiding the pitying gazes of their fellow passengers. On a sudden impulse, Maggie bolted from the crowded hold and climbed the companionway steps for one last look at her father. The Jordans had not been present at the hanging, and Maggie had not been allowed the chance to bid her father farewell. The strange, tarred figure she now saw swinging from the gibbet—surely that could not be her beloved Da. She felt no horror gazing on her father's corpse, just a sharp sense of loss, of unredeemable sadness, of incomprehension. Someday, she might be able to accept that the severity of Jordan's crimes had required such an end, but she would never be able to believe that her father was a bad man.

"Goodbye, Da," said Maggie Jordan, finally, blowing a kiss with her good hand as they passed by.

SEVERAL MONTHS AFTER THE FAMILY'S DEPARTURE, John Kelly was tried and convicted for piracy for his failure to come to John Stairs' aid on September 13, but was later pardoned; most believed that he could not be held responsible for his actions by reason of insanity. Many believed it would only be a matter of time before he succeeded in killing himself.

September 1844, Halifax—

THE EARLY MORNING SUN had not had time to warm the rocks at Black Rock Beach when the solitary young man strayed from his usual walk along the main road at Point Pleasant and ventured toward the place citizens of Halifax had been avoiding for thirty-five years. The gibbet had once stood near the road and one could not help seeing it if one desired to walk along the water's edge, where the sea breezes were the most refreshing in the summer months. The wooden structure had rotted away over the years, leaving a pile of debris strewn over the ground at the place Halifax now called Jordan's Bank. Piracy had been on everyone's mind again with the sensational capture, trial and execution of the four *Saladin* mutineers in Halifax. Perhaps because of the grotesque public disintegration of Edward Jordan's body, the *Saladin* pirates had been spared gibbeting, the usual punishment for such a crime, and were hastily buried subsequent to their hanging.

The young man's approach was tentative—from his youngest childhood, he had been warned of the punishments meted out to evildoers, murderers especially, but he was possessed of a curiosity that could not easily be contained. At last, he reached the feared place and gazed upon the remains of Jordan the pirate.

His bones had been well picked by the crows and gulls, and with age and weather, were now only scattered fragments. At a distance, weathered and almost indistinguishable from the beach pebbles that surrounded and partially buried it, was Jordan's skull, its lower jaw now broken and lost.

Hesitantly, the boy picked up the skull and turned it around in his hands, examining it carefully. So this was Ned Jordan, the feared and notorious pirate of his parents' generation! The boy could see that the city had nothing to fear from Jordan now. With great care, he wrapped the skull in two pocket handkerchiefs and placed it delicately in his satchel. He would have to hurry or he would be late for school. All through that day, he kept his satchel and its macabre contents at his desk, and forbade even his best chums a peek inside. He felt strangely protective of it, though he knew he could not keep it long.

Later, and without his parents' knowledge, he made a trip to the Mechanics' Institute, a place where he felt sure the skull would be safe. He told the librarian at the heavy oak desk where he had found the skull and that he was sure it must have belonged to the well-known pirate executed in 1809. The curator of the museum started at the name of Ned Jordan, but something in the lad's earnestness and desire to see the skull preserved made him accept it with assurances that it would not be disposed of.

Left alone with Jordan's skull after the boy had gone, the librarian realized the lad had not told him his name.

Black Rock Beach, the location where Jordan was gibbeted.
Deadman's Beach is visible in the background.

Skull of Ned Jordan, on display as part of the
Nova Scotia Museum exhibit "Pirates: Myth & Reality."